NUMBERS
COLLIDE

REBECCA RODE

ONE
LEGACY

I GAZED upon the island before me, beneath me, *around* me, and couldn't think of a single thing to say. Words would have broken the magic of it all—the gray sky that seemed to extend forever, the dark-blue water that disappeared over the horizon, the sound of the wild grass dancing softly in the breeze.

All this existed long before I did, and it would exist long after I was gone. The thought shouldn't have been comforting, but it was. No matter what happened to New NORA in these next few weeks, this—this beautiful, quiet part of the world—would live on.

"You're speechless," said Foster, my assistant. "That's a good thing, right?"

At nineteen, Foster was older than I, but sometimes he felt much younger. This was one of those times. The wind blew his dark, shoulder-length hair into his eyes, and he shoved it aside impatiently, watching my face for any hint of my thoughts.

"Uh . . ." I began, but the words still wouldn't come. I tried to pull myself back from the peaceful silence and remember why we were here. *Think like a leader, not an exhausted girl looking for respite from a life she hasn't earned and doesn't want.*

I looked again, this time with new eyes. Hawking eyes, sharp and critical. From where we stood, the island felt smaller than it truly was. I wasn't sure that these hills, green and marred only by the occasional broken and rotting structure, were what we needed for our next base of operations. The city where I grew up lay far across the channel, barely visible beneath the thick gray sky. The distance alone was a problem. It would be hard enough keeping my followers alive and safe from Alex across town these days, let alone in some broken-down wilderness across a huge body of deep, cold water.

One thing was certain—either this island made the perfect base of operations or the worst. Was it possible for something to be both?

Movement caught my eye. A furry creature watched us from the bottom of the hill. It looked so different from everything I'd seen before that I positively gaped. Not a goat, surely. A shaggy sheep with a really long neck and huge black eyes that never seemed to blink. A few others emerged from the trees and stood behind it. We'd interrupted their meal.

Either that or we were about to become their meal.

"Are those dangerous?" I asked, my heart rate picking up. My feet felt cemented to the soft ground. I couldn't have run if it meant my life.

Foster chuckled at my expression. "Forgive me, Your Honor, but . . . your brother has armed Firebrands combing the city for you, yet you're afraid of a llama?"

Llama. I vaguely remembered the term from school. Growing up in the city meant I'd petted many a cat and dog, but zoos were a thing of the past. I tried to calm my racing heart. "The Firebrands are a little less furry."

He laughed. "I wouldn't get too close. Llamas can get a little aggressive if they feel threatened. They'll chase you down or bite. Or spit."

Today's tour had taken an odd turn. "Spit?"

"Yeah. They can spit pretty far too. My grandpa had a couple in his backyard when I was a kid, before the animal-rights laws. I used to try to spit as far as they did. My mom hated it."

"Okay . . ." Keeping my eyes on the animals, I took a few steps backward despite the expanse between us, then tried to focus on the task at hand. Travers would return from his explorations any second. "It's pretty, but I'm not convinced this is the best place for us. The buildings are destroyed, and we'd be separated during an attack. What we need is a central location we can defend." Even better would be not having to defend it at all, but Alex's Firebrands were on our tail every moment of every day. Only luck had kept us from being caught so far. "Besides, it would take years to ferry everyone over here."

Foster's smile had dimmed a bit while I spoke, but now it brightened again. "I have a solution for that. The tunnel."

I looked around again, but no tunnel presented itself—just a grassy island with dozens of hills and clusters of trees. "I don't follow."

"The wealthy used to live on this island. You saw the big houses coming in, right?"

Big *destroyed* houses, yes, but I nodded anyway.

"Before the Old War, several executives left the city to settle somewhere quiet. This island was the perfect place except for one thing—they had to ferry back and forth, and that took too much time. So they built a private, two-lane underwater tunnel. When the richest of them died, his heirs turned the family house into a resort and bought the tunnel rights from their neighbors. It became one of the most popular destinations in the state—till the tunnel caved in one day, killing fifty-two people."

I flinched. What a terrible way to die.

"Old records say the tunnel was never rebuilt, but they're wrong." His earlier excitement returned full force, and he waved his hands absently as he spoke. "A private investor repaired it fifty years ago. We could bring everyone here through the tunnel, and Alex would never see them coming, especially if we do it at night. The resort has plenty of space for everyone, and it's defensible, not to mention that we'll see any intruders coming from a long way off. We'll only need to figure out how to get those old generators to work."

I couldn't help but be impressed. I should have known Foster would think of everything. He'd served Dad as an intern for two years, after all. "I see. And food options?"

"There's a bay for fishing, although we'd be seen pretty easily from the air so we'd have to be careful. And there's a storage room off the resort's kitchen. I haven't investigated yet, but I'm guessing we'll find something there too. At worst, there are hundreds of wild llamas running around. I hear they taste like a cross between beef and lamb." Foster frowned. He liked his furry childhood friends more than he let on, it seemed.

I nodded thoughtfully, pushing a windblown strand of hair behind my ear. It flopped right into my eyes again. My cabinet—consisting of Gram and two surviving councilors—expected me to form an army of the supporters who flocked to us each day. But that wasn't what my followers needed. It was food, shelter, water, and safety—

all things we'd struggled to find enough of these past weeks.

I gave up on the hair and let it whip around in the breeze, wishing I'd listened to my tutor a little more. He'd droned on about resources and survival, and I'd groaned and whined through most of it. Surely Alex was glad for his attentive listening about now. Half the city supported Alex's reign and his promise to reinstate the Rating system. The other half opposed him, but that didn't necessarily mean they supported me. They simply wanted their fallen loved ones to receive the medical attention Alex denied them. That, or they believed the rumors that I could have their implants safely removed. In both cases, providing for such a large group had become my most pressing concern.

Thankfully, our temporary hospital fulfilled the first need, though we had far more patients than our medical volunteers could handle, a problem brought to my attention daily. But there wasn't much I could do about that. The second need felt even more daunting. Millian and her brain-specialist partner, Physician Redd, had discovered how to temporarily deactivate our implants. It involved magnets and gravity, and even though I'd gone through it myself, I still didn't understand exactly how it worked.

But we all knew it wasn't a permanent solution. If Virgil ever returned from Malrain and decided to wreak havoc again, I had no doubt he could figure out how to reactivate everyone. We had to discover how to safely remove the implants. Once we did, all those patients in comas would be healed. *Dad* would be healed. We'd lost a few to Virgil's horrid update, but at least we'd save the rest.

". . . the water is fresh on that side of the island," Foster continued, and I realized he'd been talking for a while. I tried to pay better attention as he continued, naming the island's benefits as if reading down a memorized list. He'd come prepared as always, a virtue I appreciated more each day.

When he finished, I forced a smile. "Thank you for showing me. I think it's worth considering. Let's have a team of engineers investigate the tunnel's soundness and a security team check out the resort."

"Fair enough," Foster said, looking pleased.

I didn't voice my other doubts, such as whether our communications worked this far from the city or new followers could find us here. But a greater worry gripped my mind in a terrible way. Defensible or not, if Alex discovered us here or found the tunnel, he could defeat us in a single battle—one I doubted most would survive. A few weeks before, I wouldn't have assumed my brother capable of such a thing. But now, after watching Alex replace Enforcers with Firebrands and seeing my followers' homes burned to the ground in retaliation, I could no longer make assumptions. Alex wasn't the boy I'd grown up with. It was time to accept that.

"We need to go, Miss Hawking," my driver, Travers, said, his long legs striding up the hill. His frame always reminded me of a teenager's—not strong and young but lanky and awkward and somehow still growing into itself despite his wrinkles and rapidly disappearing silver hair. Perfect timing as usual. I suspected he'd hung out of sight, listening, waiting until we finished our conversation. He halted next to me. "Any word from Physician Redd yet?"

"None." I patted the old-fashioned long-distance radio in my pocket, resisting the urge to check the volume again. I'd turned it all the way up upon our arrival. My nerves fluttered in my stomach. What was it they said? The third time's a charm? Surely this time the operation would succeed. I didn't know if I could handle another patient's death, whether they would have died anyway or not. Each failure made Dad feel further away than the time before.

"Thanks, Travers." I glared back at the llama, who hadn't moved an inch since our conversation began, and began to pick my way carefully down the grassy hill. This morning's rain had made it slippery, and I nearly ended up on my backside twice before Travers wordlessly offered an elbow. It wouldn't do for my assistant to see me fall today. He was probably still laughing about the llama thing. I didn't turn around to check.

As we approached the harbor where our boat waited, a soft, orange light bathed the entire island. Our visit coincided with dusk so we could travel back under cover of darkness. Despite my worries, I found myself hoping the committee chose this location. The clean wind that rushed up from the sea smelled of new growth and salt and promise. I could almost imagine couples vacationing here long ago, walking on this very path to the harbor together, celebrating weddings or anniversaries, and even bringing children along to skip rocks on the water. The thought brought Kole back to mind, and for the first time in a while, I felt my lips lift into a tiny smile.

I'll bring Kole back here someday, I told the island silently. *No matter what.*

"Gram would like this place, I think," Travers said.

I gave the island one last sweeping look before stepping into the boat. She would. Maybe it would help her health where nothing else did. She'd taken to wearing half a dozen blankets and taking naps again. Maybe the sea air would help Dad, too, though his condition made it hard to transport him. I added that to my list of concerns. If we moved everyone out here, Physician Redd would come too. Putting

Dad in a public hospital wasn't an option with Alex searching for him. I didn't think my brother would kill our father, but then, I hadn't expected him to stage a coup and take over the country either.

Thankfully, I had a few surprises in store for him. We wouldn't be on the run much longer.

"Home, then?" Travers asked as he climbed in next to me. Foster followed, taking a seat in back.

"The warehouse, if you don't mind," I told him. "Millian is waiting to give her report."

Foster perked up. "You're going to see Director Millian?"

Travers and I looked at him in confusion. I wasn't surprised that Foster knew Millian, but they couldn't be that close. He looked like a boy with a stack of new credits, begging to go to the candy shop.

Foster clamped his mouth shut, a bit of pink staining his cheeks. "Sorry, Your Honor."

Interesting. I'd be keeping an eye on him.

Travers and I exchanged a look, and then he spoke. "It's been a long day. I'll have Millian visit you at the house."

I shook my head. "I don't want to interrupt Millian's work. What she's doing is important. And the fewer visitors at the house, the better." I glanced at Foster, who fixed his gaze on the ocean. "Besides, I want Gram to rest, and we both know she'll feel obligated to socialize if anyone drops by."

Travers gave a single, decided nod. "To the warehouse, then." He started the boat and steered us away from the dock. It was then I noticed the redness in his eyes.

"Are you all right?" I asked, leaning over so he could hear me over the wind. "You've been quiet all day."

He didn't answer right away. I knew he would reply

only when he was ready, so I waited in silence as I watched the island shrink behind us.

I was about to apologize for my question when Travers finally spoke, his voice tight. "My wife and I, we were married on the island. I don't wish to talk about it."

In the weeks since Virgil's update, many of NORA's citizens had lost loved ones. Most, like Dad, still lay in comas, but not all had received the care they needed in time. Travers's wife had died on their living room floor. He'd refused to discuss her or anything related to her. He'd even moved into the house with us. I suspected he couldn't set foot in his home with her gone.

I placed a comforting hand on his shoulder. Hopefully it was enough for him to know I understood. Travers grieved like I did, alone and quietly. His throat moved as he swallowed, but he said nothing more.

TWO
LEGACY

THE TEMPORARY HOSPITAL wasn't much to see. But, of course, that was the point. We'd repurposed a warehouse across town in the Shadow district, the part of town with worn, ill-repaired streets, broken buildings, and even more broken people. Kole's childhood home. The heavy neighborhood stench of standing water and trash made it perfect for us. Alex would never consider this neighborhood for our secret resistance laboratory. I wasn't surprised to see a new graffiti creation on one wall as we pulled up. Bright red letters, sharp and outlined in white, covered one corner.

I squinted before realizing what it said. "Rage?"

"At least it isn't profanity this time," Travers muttered.

"Rage, rage, against the dying of the light," I recited quietly, figuring it referred to the poem. My literature professor insisted it referred to death, but it always made me think of Mom. The cool darkness of night had been our special time, the moments I looked forward to most as each day closed its petals, sheltering what lay inside. Nighttime meant safety and solitude. If anything, I would rage against the stabbing intrusiveness of daylight.

"I suspect it doesn't refer to the verse," Travers said. "Most likely a Firebrand offshoot group. A younger crowd, if I dare make a guess. Dane Mason discourages his followers to leave any trace of their whereabouts."

So much for my theory. "Maybe we should finish the poem for them. Do you have any paint?"

He made a deep gurgling sound in his throat. A laugh, surely, although there was no expression as he climbed out and opened my door. It was hard to tell what Travers felt sometimes.

We went around back to the narrow side door. I fumbled with the lock, using the old-fashioned key attached to a chain around my neck, and yanked the door open. It protested with a loud creak. Millian had chosen not to fix that. "The perfect security system," she'd said.

A tiny room with sofas and a desk greeted us, looking much like a seating area for customers—a front for curious visitors, new since yesterday. Millian's team had worked into the night to secure the building, it seemed.

The second door swung open more easily. The warm wall of humidity and body odor and the shuffling, whirring, and humming of medical equipment nearly overwhelmed my senses. Only Millian's lab was visible from here. The hospital section lay beyond the far wall, keeping our most critical patients hidden from intruders. Physician Redd would be back there now, in the sterile operating room. I still hadn't received any word from him about the current patient's prognosis. I crossed my fingers. *Please let that be a good thing.*

I straightened my shoulders before striding inside, a lesson I'd learned from watching Dad. He always took a second before entering a room as His Honorable Malachite Hawking. I never understood as a child, but I did now. Presence meant everything. It did far more than ensure we Hawkings held on to our power, as the Firebrands insisted. A leader's presence meant assurance, comfort. It meant "I've got this, so you can stop worrying now."

It meant all kinds of things that weren't true for me. But like it or not, the presence was now mine to bear.

Millian stood in the corner, white coat and all, carrying her characteristic clipboard even though I knew there wouldn't be anything written on it. Her version of presence, I supposed. Her dark-brown skin gleamed with perspiration under the hot lights. She wore her black hair piled atop her head in two buns secured with ribbons, a tiny ringlet escaping down the back of her neck. Only the hospital wing was conditioned for temperature, meaning Millian's group suffered from this year's early onset of humidity. We'd made plans to ensure our security and secrecy here, but nobody had expected ventilation to become our biggest challenge.

Millian turned and grinned, her white teeth brilliant under the sharp lights overhead. "There you are. I was beginning to think you had to swim back. How was the island? Any possibility there?"

I wanted to plop myself into the nearest chair, but I noted several faces turn in our direction. Instead, I sat carefully and hid a weary sigh. This wasn't Neuromen, and we were no longer candidates competing for lab-assistant positions. Just weeks before, Millian had despised me. Now she was the friend I'd never allowed myself to have. She had this way of reading what I couldn't say and teasing the truth out of me, and as infuriating as I sometimes found that particular trait, it reminded me so much of Mom it felt as if Millian and I had always known each other. Probably the whole scientist thing.

I wasn't the only person who'd seen Millian's potential.

Within weeks, Millian had shot to the top of Neuromen's former lab specialists, becoming something of a star in their circles. She had a way of seeing the big picture in an environment where scientists often got lost in details. She also had a way with people that I envied. If I hadn't appointed her director, her coworkers would have.

Even now, I could see her hand in all of this—in the organized tables and well-trained shifts of scientists and technicians, screens full of carefully analyzed data, and calm sense of control. Yes, she understood the presence thing, but she also had the muscle to back it up.

There was no one else I trusted more to fix what Director Virgil had broken with his terrible implant update targeting his enemies. He'd already taken Mom from me. I wouldn't let him have Dad too.

Millian lifted an impatient eyebrow, and I remembered she awaited an answer.

"The island was . . . an interesting option," I said. "I'm sending teams to investigate, but I'm not sure we have the time or resources to secure it."

She pressed her lips together. "I trust your judgment, but remember that the oddest locations can mean the most safety. We need to hide where your brother won't find us. He'd never think to look there."

"Probably not, but security is only half of it. Housing a thousand people is going to be tough. We need restroom facilities and beds and kitchens and security and communications and ventilation, not to mention food that's easily stored but still nutritious and accessible."

She whistled, long and slow. "It's official. I got the easy job."

My laugh came out in one tight burst. Only Millian would think saving hundreds of patients with brain scarring was easy. "Not in the least. I'm hearing good things about your accomplishments already. Only one member of your team has issued any complaints, but I think we both know why."

Her face twisted in a wry grin, and she threw a sideways glance at one of her lab workers two tables over. The man hadn't been happy to work under a new graduate's supervision, but she'd quickly straightened him out. Though, even now, he kept his head down and shot glares in our direction.

He couldn't hear us, but I lowered my voice anyway. "Have you heard from Physician Redd yet?"

"No." She glanced at the wall. "It usually doesn't take this long."

"Then I hope you have some good news for me," I told her, eyeing the table she'd been working at. A human brain floated in a huge jar. My stomach nearly turned over. That hadn't been there yesterday either.

She didn't seem to notice my discomfort. "I do have good news, actually. Well, not news, per se, but a solid theory."

I perked up. Millian had spent a couple of weeks looking over Virgil's research and technology, gaining a basic understanding of how it interacted with the brain. But then she'd realized she wouldn't get very far without an understanding of the brain as well, so she'd recruited Physician Redd's help. Whenever the man wasn't seeing to our most critical patients or visiting the less-affected ones across town, they sat at Millian's desk and worked in hushed whispers. I tried to stamp down the hope that sprang up at her words. Even if Physician Redd's operation went poorly, if we could figure out how to heal all the affected people without removing their implants—or even how to remove them without losing the patient altogether—it would be a huge victory.

Before Millian could respond, a woman with several braids pulled into a thick ponytail approached. She ducked her head as she arrived. "Sorry to interrupt your conversation, Your Honor, but the reaction I'm recording is time-sensitive. Director Comondor, could you please give a quick authorization?"

"Of course," Millian said easily, swiping her finger across the clipboard in her hand. I leaned over to see a small screen come to life, full of data and numbers I couldn't begin to understand. The woman muttered her thanks and returned to her station.

"What's that?" I asked, gesturing to what I'd assumed to be an empty clipboard all this time.

"The master program. Stores all our data in one secure location, and it's easy to transport or hide if we get raided." She hit a few more buttons, then killed the screen. It turned white once more, its disguise nearly perfect. "I designed this the first day, and Kole helped me build it."

Kole had done that? I always forgot that my boyfriend had worked in tech assembly before declaring for Neuromen. I just shook my head in wonder.

"Okay, here's what we know about Virgil's implant," Millian said, her no-nonsense manner descending upon her once more. "First, the location is critical. It has to be placed precisely and connected to the visual and audio-circulatory centers of the brain to work." She pointed at a section of the brain on her desk, looking completely unaffected by the fact that she'd displayed the human remains like a trophy. "Second, the material of the implant is incredibly important, otherwise the brain would be poisoned within weeks. Third, we know it works on a self-charging circuit that generates heat, but so far that heat hasn't caused issues with the surrounding neurons. We don't yet know why that is. We do know the damage to the implant site, which is the BA37 in the temporal cortex, has, so far, been found irreversible. We can't heal those neurons from the outside, so we've been looking at ways to get the body to heal itself. Technically, that should happen while the patient is in the induced coma. Except it isn't."

I frowned. "That's the problem? The brain won't heal itself?"

"We've examined forty patients so far, all chosen at random. Their scans show no improvement whatsoever. It's like the patient's brain doesn't know it's broken, so it doesn't set to work on those neurons."

"So what does that mean exactly?

"It means something is wrong, and it can't be natural."

Nothing about implants was natural, but I didn't argue the point. "So you think Virgil did something to the implants to prevent healing."

"I think it's blocking it, yes. Once we find it, those patients' prognoses should immediately improve."

"And if you don't find it?"

Millian bit her lip.

Got it. "You'll find it. I know you will." I found my hands clenching and forced them to relax. She had to find the solution, or it would be Dad on that operating table soon enough.

"You can count on that," Millian said easily. "I won't rest until we have answers."

By the look of the cot next to her desk, the blankets still folded in their original plastic packaging, she wasn't lying. "You're eating the meals I've sent over, right?"

"Some of them." She paused. "Hey, I don't know if

you've seen our lovely new art outside, but we've had some visitors lately. I think the neighborhood is on to us. Any way we can increase security around here? If the power gets cut, we won't accomplish much at all."

We'd chosen this warehouse—an old food-packaging plant—because it circumvented the city's rolling blackouts. Constant electricity meant constant work, and that was exactly what we needed when every day was critical. But Millian was right—if somebody got curious and decided to do some damage, we'd be in serious trouble.

I added it to my already-too-long list. "We're already stretched pretty thin, but I'll see what I can do."

"Thanks." She'd already turned back to her work, half present. It was a state I remembered in Mom, and it made my throat hurt.

Standing up, I watched her for a second and then headed for the hospital door. Mom would have liked Millian. Kole, though . . . I wasn't sure about, and, strangely enough, I didn't care. Kole was the one thing in my life I'd truly chosen for myself. He wasn't the rich, privileged boy my parents would have wanted, but I already knew plenty about boys like that. Kole didn't care about my heiress status. If anything, it put distance between us— a distance I was perfectly willing to cross if it meant keeping us together. Kole was worth it. He would always be worth it.

The door opened just before I reached it, and Physician Redd stepped out. As my heart leaped into a gallop, I felt my stomach cramp just a bit. The exhaustion on his face told me all I needed to know.

"I'm sorry," he said.

I didn't know the patient, but that didn't matter. What did matter was that someone had entrusted their family member to us and we'd failed them. Nausea joined the cramping in my stomach.

"Are we any closer?" I managed.

"I don't know," he murmured.

There was deep disappointment in the man's tired eyes. His hair looked grayer and thinner than before all this began. What would he look like in a few more weeks, after more failed operations and more deaths? What would that do to all of us?

"Go home and rest," I told him. "We'll talk about it tomorrow."

He dipped his head. "Thank you, Your Honor. Although . . . I didn't come out to report on the procedure. There's something else we need to discuss." His frown sagged deeper.

More bad news? My heart practically sprinted now. "Is my dad okay?"

"He's stable. Doing better than most of my patients. He should be able to remain with you in that safe house for a while yet. Actually, I want to talk to you about Kole Mason."

My relief at Dad's condition froze at the mention of Kole's name. "The medics examined him last week. He's doing fine." I'd even seen him yesterday at his apartment, and he seemed perfectly normal—as normal as an overly paranoid and overprotective boyfriend could be, anyway. I wanted him to stay with us, but he insisted on keeping an apartment several miles away, muttering something about the Firebrands wanting his head—yet another reason this war needed to end. I couldn't wait for us to settle down together like a real couple.

I tried to imagine us living like that, each going to our respective jobs every morning—me to the Copper Office and him to the tech assembly center like he'd always intended to do—and then eating dinner together at the Hawking family table at the end of the day. It was disturbingly hard to imagine.

Physician Redd cleared this throat. "The medics didn't have his latest brain scan. I do." He shoved a clipboard much like Millian's into my hand and swiped the tech screen until it displayed a grayish mass. Several angry red messages appeared, the top one flashing in bold letters.

"Look right there," he said, pointing at what had to be the back and center of Kole's brain. I saw nothing but a dense cloud, but he didn't wait for me to express my confusion. "The damage is far more extensive than in the others—not in intensity but in surface area."

"You showed me that already," I said. He'd shown me Kole's results before he even gained consciousness the first time. "So it isn't healing?"

"The others aren't healing, but Kole's condition is even more concerning. Somehow, and I don't know how, the damage is getting worse."

I stared at the image, my legs suddenly feeling a little tingly. It couldn't be getting worse when Kole seemed perfectly normal. "How is that possible?"

"Environmental factors, perhaps. Or stress. This is something I've never seen before, to be honest." He stepped aside to allow a medical assistant through the door, her arms wrapped around a bucket of supplies. She ducked her head respectfully as she passed me, her expression somber, the heavy scent of blood following her like death. I caught a glimpse of fabric and plastic and a bit of clothing in the bucket, all stained bright red.

I looked away.

"What do we do about it, then?" I whispered. "Surgery? An induced coma? Bed rest?"

"Removing scar tissue this extensive would kill him. A coma could slow the progression, but it's hard to know for sure. For now, I would watch him carefully. If he starts to act erratically or his speech becomes slurred, let me know right away."

I nodded a little too quickly. "Okay."

"I'm sorry," he said again. He hesitated as if wanting to say something else, then shook his head and walked back through the door.

I stood frozen in place for a minute, struggling to control my quick breaths. So much for the composure thing. I must have looked like a disaster.

Virgil's horrible "experiment" with the brain implants had nearly cost Kole his life. Physician Redd had recommended a coma at first, saying his brain needed rest, but Kole always refused. He wouldn't consider it even now, no matter the evidence. Kole had always been stubborn about his independence. Even if a coma would help, how was I supposed to convince him to submit to a needle, sleep through the apocalypse, and wake up when it was all over?

There was no way he'd agree to that. Ever.

"Is something wrong, Miss Hawking?" Travers asked, and I realized he'd crossed the room to stand by my side and watch me fall apart. Several pairs of eyes watched from behind him. Technicians and scientists paused in their work, sensing the gravity of my conversation with the physician. Everyone in the lab had to know the stakes of today's operation. Thanks to my demeanor, they would also know the outcome.

"Nothing's wrong," I lied, unable to hide the waver in my voice.

Presence.

Travers looked at me with concern, but he didn't challenge my words. He watched as I straightened my shoulders once more, lifted my chin, and assumed the demeanor of a Hawking leader. Now I was a fake on the inside *and* the outside.

"Should we head home, then?" my driver asked gently.

I considered it for a moment. I could tell Kole I was too tired to meet tonight. He would understand. But that would mean another sleepless night, worrying and wishing I'd told him. It was his brain. He deserved to know, didn't he?

That familiar clutch of nausea told a different story. It wasn't benevolence that drove me to meet him now. It was pure and utter selfishness. I needed Kole. How had I allowed myself to care so deeply, so fast? Especially when everyone in my life had abandoned me in one form or another. I should have known I would lose him too.

I moved forward on shaky legs, feeling anger replace the fear. Good. Anger was good. Anger would help me function where grief would break me.

"Not home," I said. "I need to speak with Kole."

THREE
KOLE

Legacy's transport pulled up just as I arrived home. I slipped into the shadows next to the apartment building's porch before she could see me. I wanted to surprise her, but I also wanted to prevent any neighbors from seeing us together. For her protection, not mine. I'd much rather they came out and confronted me if they had a problem. People like that were much easier to deal with than the sneaky types.

Another bonus—the darkness also hid my face. I fingered my sore eye and winced at the swelling. The Firebrand I'd confronted today initially looked like Zenn, one of my best friends, and I'd been excited to see him before I remembered the truth. We weren't on the same team anymore. If you considered politics, we weren't on the same planet anymore.

But alas, it hadn't been Zenn but a strange face with the same tattoo I wore. That guy would never wander the city alone again after today. A blessing and a curse. The smarter they got, the harder it became to get the information I needed. After two run-ins and narrow escapes, I still couldn't confirm that the arsonists burning down the homes belonging to Legacy's followers were indeed Firebrands, as I suspected.

Not that I needed proof. It had my Uncle Dane's name written all over it.

Travers opened Legacy's door, and she slipped out. She wore her long brown hair down over her shoulders in a tangled mess I longed to run my fingers through. As always, she strode toward me like a woman who knew her path, her form slender and athletic, a leader certain of her place in the world. But unlike always, there was a grim set to her mouth that stole the smile from my lips. The visit to the island hadn't gone well, then.

"Still getting driven around, princess?" I teased, stepping out of the shadows just as Legacy reached the set of double doors.

She whirled, placing a hand on her chest, and gasped. "You scared the daylights out of me."

"Speaking of daylight, are you sure you should be driving around the city right now? You could have been seen."

"Spare me the lecture. I had to see you." She threw herself into my arms. A tiny thrill shot through me even though we'd embraced like this hundreds of times in the past few weeks. Embraced, and talked, and kissed, and laughed, and kissed again. I thought of Legacy's soft lips and our hours together more often than I wanted to admit. I still couldn't believe this was real, that Legacy Hawking, of all people, so thoroughly consumed my life. Yet somehow, it felt like it had always been this way.

I breathed her in, feeling the world settle into some resemblance of rightness for the first time all day. She smelled of sea wind and a tangy shampoo I didn't recognize, and she clung to me more tightly than usual. Definitely a hard day. I'd have to distract her, then.

"I feel bad for Travers," I said, watching her driver and transport pull away. He would find a safe place to park for a while, then return for her in an hour or so. Parking such a vehicle out front was too dangerous in this neighborhood.

"Well, I don't plan to drive myself around until I have to," she said in a joking tone. "I'm a Hawking, aren't I?"

Some of the amusement left her eyes as we both realized the implication in her words. Yes, she was a Hawking, but . . . she also wasn't. Not in the sense that her grandmother, Treena Hawking, intended when she set up the line of succession. Legacy's adopted status was Alex's biggest argument against Legacy from taking the throne, and probably the only one he could have made that anyone agreed with. If Legacy's parents had announced the adoption from the beginning, people would be accustomed to the idea. But now the entire country seemed split down the middle—some calling her an imposter with a questionable past and aligning themselves with Alex, others calling her the rightful heir to the throne and coming to her for aid. The former claimed Alex's parentage indisputable, a point the latter struggled to argue with. The fact that her father wanted her in charge rather than Alex didn't seem to matter.

Of course, with her dad in a coma, it was also impossible to prove.

"You know that people from the Shadows don't have drivers, right?" I said against her hair. "Especially the same one every time they leave the house. Eventually someone will recognize Travers and make the connection."

Legacy seemed oddly stiff as she pulled away. "I know, but Gram refuses to let me go anywhere alone, and he's better than a jumpy guard. Besides, he's been so down lately. This job is the one thing he has left. I can't take it away from him."

I felt a stab of sympathy for the poor man. His wife passed away during the first wave of implant-update deaths a few weeks before, leaving him looking utterly lost. I knew that feeling well. "You can't fix everything. I admire that you try anyway, though." I brushed Legacy's hair aside and gave her a gentle kiss on the forehead.

She snorted. "I come across town to see you, and that's all I get?"

I raised my hands in surrender. "Hey, we're outside, and there could be people walking b—"

She yanked my head down for a long kiss—a firm, decisive one. It felt as if she were angry, and I couldn't deny the heat sparking between us. Maybe a good thing, the fact that we were still outside. Then she pulled away, leaving me a puddle at her feet. She stared at me, her deep brown eyes looking deep into my own. A second later, she groaned, placing one soft finger to my bruised temple. "You got into another fight, didn't you?"

I swore silently. "This one wasn't my fault."

"Right. Let me guess. The other guy walked right into your fist."

"I tried to talk him down. He didn't like it."

She took a step back and put a hand on her hip, wearing an expression that clearly said, *I don't believe you.*

"It isn't my first black eye, nor will it be the last. No big deal. Clearly you didn't grow up in the Shadows."

I'd kept my tone light, but Legacy continued to stare me down. This couldn't be about the fight with that Firebrand. Something definitely bothered her today. "What's wrong? Did something happen?"

She opened her mouth, closed it, and sighed. "It's just all the fighting, and now you too. How am I supposed to bring peace to a country at war with itself in every possible way?"

"We aren't a bunch of children you have to reprimand, Legacy. You keep saying you want change. You forget that change requires a little pain."

She gave me a long look. "Fear doesn't change hearts. Improvement happens from the inside out, not the outside in."

I thought about the fear on that Firebrand's face and winced inwardly before reminding myself whose side he'd been on. Dane and his pups deserved no sympathy from me. "Yeah, well, sometimes it has to start on the outside or it doesn't happen at all. Don't worry. I have everything under control."

She folded her arms—not a good sign. "I can't worry about you, but you can worry about me? Is that how this is supposed to work?"

"Exactly. I'm glad you're finally getting it. Now, where were we?"

The sternness melted a bit, and she punched my shoulder, her frown melting into a lopsided grin. "I think we were discussing what really happened with whoever decorated your face."

"Actually, I think we were discussing moving this conversation upstairs."

Legacy made a face—she hated when I changed the subject on her—but she followed me inside and up the creaky stairs. As always, I flinched as I entered my apartment, seeing it from her perspective. I'd already cleaned it as best I could, but there was no hiding the lack of food in the refrigerator. Hopefully she wouldn't check.

"It isn't just the bruise," she said as I closed the front door and locked it. "How do you explain the black circles under your eyes?"

Time for another distraction because this was a topic I didn't want to discuss right now. I wrapped my arms around her again and let my hands slide down to her slim waist. "Can you blame me? I mean, being without you for a whole day is hard on a guy."

She leaned against me and placed a slender finger on my lips. "I'm serious. You look like you haven't slept in days. Is it the nightmares?"

They weren't nightmares, exactly. More like intense, twisted memories, mostly of the day my implant nearly killed me, although the occasional childhood memory returned. Sometimes it was Dane beating me, other times Virgil or my father or those Neuromen thugs. Even worse were the dreams with Dad. Those lingered long after I woke. I could never admit to Legacy how bad they messed with my head.

Legacy frowned at my expression. "That's what I thought."

I pulled away and crossed the room, keeping my back to her. "I don't need drugs, if that's where this is headed."

"If you can't sleep, maybe you do."

Here we go again. "I can sleep. I'm just under a lot of pressure right now. All of us are."

Her hands slid around my midsection from behind, and she laid her head against my back. I covered her hands with my own. "Maybe talking to someone about your mother's death will help you believe you aren't to blame."

"This isn't guilt," I shot back, feeling her hands tighten in response. Then I forced my voice to soften. "Dane is the one who killed my mom. He's the one who will pay for it."

Her hands were rigid against my chest now, her body tense.

I sighed and turned around, taking her into my arms again. It felt like we fought more often than not lately. "I'm sorry. I don't mean to be doom and gloom all the time. It's just . . . you know."

"You lost your mom, left your uncle, and now your friends have turned against you. I get it. I'm glad you chose me, and us, but it can't be easy."

"You're wrong. Being with you is the easiest thing in the world. It's everything else that's hard." I placed a finger beneath her chin, lifting her face to mine, and let myself get lost in her. I loved kissing Legacy Hawking. She wasn't timid like many girls. She knew what she wanted, and she demanded exactly that much and no less. The sparks between us were a bonfire now, an electric surge that left me utterly powerless to resist.

The rapid knock at the door sounded like a gunshot.

We leaped apart. Legacy's eyes were wide, her face red, her hair a mess where my hand had

held her a second before. Nobody ever knocked. Only Legacy's followers knew where I lived, which meant this could be a perfectly innocent interruption or a really bad thing.

I slipped between Legacy and the door, grateful I'd locked it on the way in. "Who is

it?"

"Sorry to bother you," a man's voice called, "but I have a message for Legacy Hawking."

I looked at Legacy, who frowned. The voice wasn't familiar to her either, and none of her guards would ever shout her name aloud in a public place. I cringed at the thought of my neighbors overhearing this conversation.

Legacy opened her mouth as if to respond, but I shushed her and turned back to the door. "You're kidding, right? I live here alone. Who is this again?"

"My name is Chadd," the intruder said, not sounding deterred at all. "I have a message from Legacy's mother."

Now Legacy's face drained of color, going from flushed to pale in a matter of seconds.

Anger grew within me. How dare some stranger play with her emotions like that? Her mother had been dead barely a year.

"You have the wrong apartment, *friend*," I snapped. "Best try the other end of town with all the other rich people."

"I know she's here. I watched you two enter a few minutes ago. I assure you, there's nothing to fear from me. I really am a friend, and I'm alone, but I can't go until I've delivered my message. Kadee Steer would only send me right back."

Legacy went rigid. She knew the name. Along with the shock and the horror in her eyes came a new emotion, one more chilling than the others. Hope.

I couldn't bear to see it, not when she'd already been through so much. As for the guy's promise of being alone and harmless, I was no fool. This imposter wouldn't cross my threshold as long as Legacy was under my protection.

"You have one minute to leave the building," I called out, "or I'll toss you down the stairwell myself. Starting now."

"Kole!" Legacy snapped.

The volume of Legacy's retort made me flinch. I motioned for her to hide, but she only glared at me.

Upon hearing her voice, the guy began pounding again.

"Legacy Hawking! Just let me deliver my message and I'll be on my way. I swear it."

"Say it through the door and be gone," I growled.

"It's to be given face-to-face. I'm sorry, but those were my orders. Kadee was rather insistent." A pause. "Look, you can keep your stunner on me the whole time if you like. I know about the one in your pocket."

If the words were meant to assure or disarm, they had the opposite effect. Suddenly I was very done with our visitor and this conversation.

I pushed Legacy behind the door, drawing a surprised yelp from her, whipped my stunner out, and opened the door a crack. The intruder looked a few years older than us and had blond hair, a slender form, and terrible posture. He didn't look like much of a threat, but then, most spies didn't.

He gave a start as I aimed the stunner at him. I'd expected to see a mass of Firebrands or at least a single guy with the barrel of a stun gun leveled at my face. Instead, the intruder frowned at my weapon and took off down the steps, taking them three at a time.

I looked around for accomplices but found nobody, at least in the hallway. That meant nothing. I'd be walking Legacy to her transport tonight, and she wouldn't be returning here anytime soon. I swore. This meant I'd have to find a new place to live. I didn't expect to be compromised so quickly, and worse, so easily.

I shoved the door closed and bolted it, then turned to find Legacy staring me down.

"What?" I asked.

"You really have no idea why I'm upset, do you?" she shot back, her voice trembling with barely contained anger.

Of course she wanted to fight about this. Didn't she see

the danger she'd put herself in? "We've been discovered, and you aren't safe. That's all that matters."

"Is it?"

Her question felt like a trap, so I didn't answer. I ducked around her to the window, cautiously surveying the front walk. Seconds later, the intruder stalked toward the street, turned, and disappeared. No figures emerged from the shadows to join him.

She grabbed my arm and whirled me around. "You threw me behind the door."

"For your protection. I wasn't about to leave you exposed."

"I'm not interested in being shielded. I have Travers for that, and he's unbearable enough. Did it occur to you that I might want to talk to that guy? That he might have some of the answers I've been looking for?"

That made me pause. I hadn't known she was looking for anything at all, but her safety mattered more. I had to help her understand. "Think about it. He knew I had a stunner, and he knew you were here with me. That guy has all the signs of a creepy stalker. If you can't see that, then it's a good thing I was here."

"So you could talk over me and make my decisions for me? That isn't what I need, Kole. That isn't what we're supposed to be."

I felt the blood rushing to my head and the too-familiar pain of an approaching headache. "Oh? What am I supposed to do, then, princess? Bow and let the intruder in? Give him some royal tea?"

"Don't be ridiculous." She folded her arms for the second time that night. "He knew my biological mother's name. Dad sealed those records a long time ago. He can't possibly be lying."

"Or someone found those records and waited till the right moment to take advantage," I pointed out. "Look, this mysterious message could be Alex's doing. What if he's trying to lure you outside so he can arrest you again and kill the resistance movement once and for all?"

She growled in frustration and stalked across the room. "Even if that were the case, I wanted to talk to him. I want to know how he got that information. I want to make the decision for myself because it involves *my* life, Kole. Mine."

The pressure began to build behind my eyes. This was where every argument ended up—her and her life, not us and ours. "Don't you get it? We can't trust anyone but each other. Not your selfish brother, not my Firebrand friends. Those followers who claim to be on your side? They're using you, and you can't even see it. So, no, I'm not turning you over to some stranger, no matter who he claims to know, and it isn't fair of you to ask that of me. I won't put you at risk."

The flush returned to her cheeks, but my retort seemed to stop her. She examined me for a long moment before replying, her voice soft, "Do you really see the world that way?"

The sudden gentleness in her demeanor reminded me of the medics who'd cared for me when I awoke after my ordeal with Virgil. I could see it in their eyes, hear it in their voices, imagine it in their whispers. *Poor boy. Survived an attack from a madman but lost his mother. Must be terrible living all alone in the world.* I could endure pity from strangers, though just barely. But I refused to take it from Legacy. Never her.

"I see the world as it really is," I snapped, taking a step backward. "It's you who grew up with gold silverware and feather pillows and fancy transports."

She flinched.

I remembered my earlier words and let the anger die, although the headache remained. Legacy and I were in this together. It wouldn't solve anything to remind her of our differences, and fates knew we had plenty of those.

"Look," I began again. "I know you'd love to have long-lost family members inviting you into their lives since your own family is so broken right now, but you have to consider that your enemies will know that too. I guarantee that whatever that guy intended for you, it wasn't good."

She looked insulted. "Of course I'll consider that. And you have to consider that you just prevented me from receiving an important message that mattered to me." She crossed the space between us and looked up at me, betrayal in her eyes. "I want to be with you, but not like this. Being with you is the most freedom I've ever had. I refuse to let you put me in a cage like everyone else."

"You know that's not what I want either." I stepped forward to pull Legacy into my arms again. But instead of melting against my chest like she usually did, she stood rigidly, body tense. I looked down to find her staring wistfully at the doorway.

"Do you feel angrier lately?" she asked quietly. "Or violent, maybe?"

Now I was the one who stiffened. "There's nothing wrong with me. This is who I am. As long as we're together, I will protect you whether you like it or not."

She pushed away and headed for the door.

I hurried over, blocking her exit. "Whoa, hold on. You can be angry with me all you want, but you aren't going out there alone. That guy could be hiding, waiting for you. There could be others."

"Kole."

"They would overpower me and your driver in seconds if it meant getting to you. We have to think this through. Wait until I've had a good look around—"

"Kole." She looked me straight in the eye. "Let. Me. Go."

"It isn't safe," I said stubbornly.

"Let me go, right now, or we're through."

I stared at her. Her threat echoed between us, replaying in my head. "You can't be serious."

"I wouldn't joke about this. I'll call Travers when I get outside." She patted her pocket, where I knew she hid her short-range radio. "We'll talk tomorrow."

My jaw clenched. She met my gaze with a determined stare of her own. Only Legacy would threaten to end a relationship over her boyfriend trying to save her life.

A rough day, I assured myself. *That's all it is. She'll come to her senses tomorrow.*

"Fine," I said in a nonchalant tone. "But I'm going first." I stepped outside and closed the door behind me before she could say a word. Then I slid my stunner out and checked every possible hiding place in the hallway and stairwell. Not a soul, even outside. At least none of my neighbors had heard the intruder's yelling.

I was on my third pass around the dead lawn when Legacy stalked out. She reached the sidewalk just as Travers pulled up.

"All clear, princess," I growled just loudly enough for her to hear. Deep down, I knew I was being a jerk, but she wasn't exactly helping things either.

She didn't spare me a glance, just yanked the transport door open and launched herself inside. The door slammed shut as the vehicle sped away and vanished into the darkness.

FOUR
KOLE

Somewhere in my nightmares, I knew two things: darkness surrounded me, and the darkness was hot.

Thick blackness clogged my throat and lungs like smoky tar. It wouldn't go away no matter how hard I coughed.

I threw myself free of the mattress and hit the floor, hard. Orange light flickered from beneath the door, revealing a black cloud pouring in around the doorframe. No wonder I couldn't breathe. Hot tears forced my eyes into rapid blinking, and my ears refused to clear. Then I realized it wasn't my ears—it was the sound of flames devouring my living room.

This was no dream.

Alarm slapped my mind awake. My door was all that kept me alive right now. My only exit would be the window, but fire escapes didn't exist in the Shadows. The buildings had insurance to back their worth, but human beings didn't. Anyone poor enough to live here wasn't worth saving.

Something crashed on the other side of the door. Part of the roof?

The window it is.

I threw the window open so hard the glass rattled in its frame. The fresh air made me gasp. I stood there, panting, looking at the long drop below as the black smoke billowed out past me.

I could jump to the ground four stories below. I *might* live through it. It would just break both my legs and probably my neck while I was at it. It would take Dane all of twenty-four hours to discover me at the hospital and finish me off. A flash of memory returned—my mom with Dane's knife in her chest and the life draining from her eyes. I had no desire to repeat that scene from a gurney.

No. Jumping and taking a chance on my life wasn't an option. The roof, then. There had to be a section that hadn't caught fire yet.

I turned around and pulled myself up by the window frame. An extension of rooftop jutted out above me, the one benefit of living on the top floor. I grabbed it and immediately jerked my hand away. Even the shingles felt like molten tar. The fire had spread far beyond my living room.

Several slams echoed in the night as others opened their own windows. One woman screamed for help on the floor beneath me, her voice shrill and terrified. I looked down and swore.

Not a woman. A child. She couldn't be older than eight or nine.

I ran through my options, which had seriously begun to dwindle by this point, and made a quick decision. As bad as ending up in the hospital seemed, abandoning a kid would be worse.

I adjusted my grip on the windowsill and set my sights downward, lowering my body with shaking arms until my toes reached the top lip of the girl's window frame. Now for the hard part. I grabbed a drain pipe that ran beneath my window, and when it began to pull away from the wall, I balanced most of my weight on my toes. A deep breath, and I lowered myself to the windowsill. My grip slipped a bit from perspiration, but I took a few short breaths, coughed, and continued on. Soon I crouched on her windowsill, grabbing the frame for support.

"Climb onto my back!" I shouted to the girl.

She pulled back and wrapped her arms around herself. As her arms moved, I saw what I hadn't been able to see before. Another face, and even more afraid. A little brother, perhaps two or three years old. Somewhere inside, a massive crash shook the building.

My lips released a torrent of curses now. From the sound of it, their parents weren't coming to get them.

I extended an arm. "Can you hold on?"

Her eyes went wide, and she pulled back again.

Great. Just as I lifted one foot to slide inside after her, the building shook again. I grabbed for the window frame with both hands but missed and found myself falling, scrambling to find something to catch me, *something*—

And one hand caught the windowsill.

I reached up with the other and hung there, my legs trembling and my breath coming in quiet gasps. Just above me, muffled sobs came from the children, who watched with round, horrified eyes. They knew the same thing I did—I'd nearly plummeted to the ground alone. How was I supposed to help two kids reach the ground safely?

A long wail sounded in the distance. The fire team. Finally. A crowd gathered below, and several of the neighbors I'd spent the past weeks avoiding watched with upturned, anxious faces. A glance up revealed a bright orange light coming through my bedroom window. My room was now aflame. That meant we didn't have much time here either. The fire team would be here in a few minutes, but those were minutes these kids didn't have.

I gripped the sill with both hands, alarmed at the shaking in my fingers. "I need you to climb onto my shoulders," I called up to the girl. "Can you do that?"

She shook her head.

"We need to help your brother get out," I said, switching tactics. "If you can lower him down to me, I'll hold him while you climb onto my shoulders. Are you willing to try?"

She paused but then nodded shyly.

"Good. Now, it's time to be really strong. I know you can do this. Lift him out, but hold on to his arms really tight."

The boy cringed as she wrapped her arms around him from behind and lifted him with a grunt. Then his legs and a couple of tiny bare feet appeared.

I ordered my grip to hold and reached upward, guiding him down, then placed his arms around my neck, feeling his legs curl around my ribs. I lifted my knee upward to help support his weight.

"Hold on tight," I told him. "Don't let go of my neck no matter what."

He gave a tiny sob and buried his face in my chest.

I looked upward at the girl, ready to tell her to climb onto my back, but my entire body trembled from exertion now. My fingers felt like they were coated in butter and slid backward no matter how hard I gripped. I could barely hold my weight, let alone the boy's. If I added any more weight, we'd all be done for.

The girl must have seen the fear on my face because she started to weep.

"I'll take the boy!" a woman called out from below, and

I felt hands grabbing my legs, guiding them to the next windowsill down. Then she extended her arms. "Slide him down. I won't let him fall."

I believed her. It was my own arms I didn't trust. But I nodded and peeled the boy's arms off my neck one-handed. "Hold on to my leg now," I told him, and he wrapped himself around it like the baby monkeys in the old zoo videos.

It took a minute to ease him down, but the woman finally grabbed him. His weight lifted from me, and I took a second to wipe the perspiration off my fingers before looking upward at the girl. My precarious perch on the hot window frame below me wouldn't hold forever. My legs trembled. The girl's eyes were anchored on her brother, making sure he reached safety. I heard a shout as a bearded man positioned himself below us, calling to the woman, offering to catch the boy. A two-story drop instead of three. It could mean the difference between life and death.

Something collapsed above us, sending a cloud of deadly smoke and hot debris showering onto my head. The girl yelped and ducked back inside as I lowered my head to protect my face, pieces of the collapsing roof singeing my scalp. The building shuddered and groaned, an awful, soulless cry, like a wounded animal approaching death. It sent goose bumps across my flesh despite the incredible heat.

"Your turn," I shouted up to the girl.

Her face appeared again. She sent a quick look inside, as if waiting for her parents, then swung down and stepped onto my shoulders, sliding down to wrap her arms around my neck like her brother had. Her weight hadn't quite settled yet when an explosion of massive heat tore my hands from the windowsill.

There was nothing but air.

The girl shrieked, clutching me tighter, closing off what little air supply I had. I flailed, grabbing for the sill again, all the while knowing I was falling and the girl would fall with me and I couldn't save her after all.

Something snapped tight around my waist.

My hand found something hard and solid—a windowsill?—and we slammed into the building once again, eliciting a yelp from the girl and a grunt from me. I grabbed the sill with my other hand and hung, panting and staring upward incredulously. The window I'd perched above just a second earlier was just above us now. I barely felt the scrapes along my legs and feet for the realization that I was alive.

Then I understood the source of our salvation—a bedsheet wrapped around my waist. The second-floor woman must have thrown it around me earlier. As I fell backward, she'd yanked hard enough to pull us back. Even now, I saw the effort in her red face as she grunted, her entire body shaking, hovering just inches above us. Had she wrapped the sheet around a bedpost for leverage? Smart woman.

She'd probably intended to use this for her own escape. I shot her a grateful smile, one she returned with a shaky grin.

"Tell me when you're ready, and I'll take the girl," the bearded man called from below.

A few breaths to calm myself, and I helped the girl down. Through the hot, black smoke and my warm tears, I caught a glimpse of him catching the girl and carrying her across the lawn to the street, where he set her down next to her crying brother. They wrapped their arms around one another. As the man strode back to us, I turned to the woman above me.

"Your turn," I called to her, reaching upward.

Then the building exploded.

I LOOKED up at the night sky. I felt something soft beneath me. I took in a long, deep breath of clean air and winced at the sharp pain that followed. The ground below me felt wet and, oh, so very cold against my burned and scraped skin.

A man's face appeared above me, his mouth moving as if yelling, but no sound emerged. Then I realized I could hear nothing but a faint, persistent, muffled ringing. I shoved the man's face away and sat up—or tried to, as my body refused to cooperate—and let my eyes focus on the odd lump of soft and hard beneath me.

A body.

I scrambled to my feet, or tried to anyway, and ended up on my backside again. The bearded man's eyes lay open, distant, and sightless. From the angle of his head, I knew he wouldn't be seeing anything ever again.

It all came back, and I turned to the pulsing, glowing mass of orange light and smoke. Only a massive pile of rubble remained where my building had just been. Debris covered the lawn. No, not debris. Bodies covered in dirt and blood. Black, brown, red, and gray—all too clear under the bright moon.

My hearing pulsed, returning in slow bursts of sound. Shuddering sobs sounded in slices from several of the spectators. The boy I'd just helped wailed from the street, his hand held by his dumbstruck older sister. I released a long breath, grateful they were both fine. I searched the frantic crowd with growing dread. The woman who'd helped the three of us was nowhere to be seen.

Several of the figures on the lawn sat up, groaning, their voices muffled. I counted them and quickly did the math. Four stories, four apartments each. There must be two or three dozen people still unaccounted for.

The shaking in my body turned violent, and suddenly I was cold despite the wave of heat emanating from the building.

So many deaths.

I held my side, testing a deep breath. Probably a bruised or cracked rib or two. My body felt pummeled, and my lungs wouldn't be the same for a long time. But I was alive. I shot another glance at the man who'd cushioned my fall, feeling a pang of regret. I chose to believe he'd been dead before I landed. I couldn't handle the alternative right now.

"That fire spread way too fast to be natural," someone said, the voice sounding far away as my ears adjusted. In the distance, the fire team transport pulled up. "I've seen dead trees burn slower than that. Foul play here. I'm sure of it."

Now that I could focus on something other than survival, a nagging suspicion gripped my senses. Foul play indeed. That Chadd guy? He could have pretended to run away and then come back to set the fire. But why announce himself first?

I shook my head. If he did this, it was under someone else's direction. And I knew exactly who that someone was. This would make the eleventh arsonist attack in seven weeks, and only one person in this city was greedy enough to kill a building of innocents just to make a point.

"You win, Uncle," I muttered into the night. "Let's play."

FIVE

LEGACY

I ABSENTLY PULLED the crust off my toast in one long piece, then tossed it onto the plate. I hadn't taken the crust off my bread like this since my dress-wearing phase at age five. Apparently, my lack of sleep was sending my brain spiraling into childhood.

The kitchen around me offered no answers. It stood still and quiet, just as hours before when I gave up on sleep and crept downstairs past Gram's sleeping door guard, Bernard. Everyone in the house slept except the person who actually needed brainpower today. By lunchtime, a dozen or more new supporters would find my scouts and join our cause. By dinner, I would receive a lecture from my cabinet about training my followers for battle. They didn't realize I had a different plan, one that didn't involve arming those who only wanted to protect their families. Any day now, General Knox would arrive from the border to assist us. Then we'd storm the Block, take the Copper Office back, and throw Alex and his Firebrands behind bars.

Meanwhile, Millian would discover how to heal the affected citizens, and Physician Redd would unravel the mystery of implant removal. I would take control until Dad awoke, and all would return to normal.

But until then, I'd suffer one sleepless night after another, worrying about all the things that could possibly go wrong while my brother hunted me like a rabbit.

"I hate this," I muttered to the empty kitchen.

"That's because it's old bread," Travers said from the bottom of the stairwell. "There's a better loaf in the pantry. In fact, let me make you a new piece. Toast is the one thing I excel at cooking." What remained of his still-wet gray hair glistened, his chin freshly shaven. He wore civilian clothes again today—trousers with a casual collared shirt—although I knew he preferred Dad's black uniform. I'd had to order him to wear something less conspicuous or he wouldn't be driving me anywhere.

To a stranger, Travers looked every inch the stiff driver this morning. But I saw the redness in his eyes. Travers hadn't slept much either.

I tossed the uneaten toast onto my plate and sighed. "I'm not really hungry."

"Couldn't sleep?"

Not at all. That response would earn me a one-way ticket back to bed, so I just said, "I have a lot on my mind."

He watched me, weighing my response. "Are you ready to talk about what happened with Kole?"

I shook my head. That made the third time he'd asked me that question since I dove into the transport last night, but my answer would remain the same for some time yet. I still didn't know what to make of Kole's strange behavior last night. Protectiveness was one thing, but he'd acted almost irrationally. Paranoid. Like he and I stood against the world, including everyone I loved.

He'd acted exactly as Physician Redd warned he would.

Travers crossed the old carpet, eyed my plate, and gave me a wry smile. "I know exactly what you need. A nice, peaceful drive. I'll fetch some of the guards outside to come along."

"No guards," I said quickly. "But a drive sounds perfect."

THE PARK before us was as quiet as our safe house had been. A bright line of sunlight moved toward us with the rising sun. The sky looked almost blue today. A clear day for once. But, for some reason, it only added to the weight I carried in my chest, especially when I looked at the dull, gray morph of a metal statue in the center of the park.

Travers ordered the transport to park behind an abandoned truck to hide it from view. Then he turned around in his seat.

"I thought we were going for a drive," I said, pretending I didn't already know exactly where this conversation was headed.

"We did. Now we're stopping."

"Because I haven't visited Mom's statue yet," I guessed.

He gave me a long look. "I know grief when I see it."

Folding my arms, I sat back in my seat. Disappointment added weight to the pain in my chest. Travers may have misinterpreted the source of my silence this morning, but he was dead on about the grief.

I refused to believe Physician Redd could be right about Kole. The expression on my boyfriend's face as he suffered under Virgil's brutal attack returned to my mind, making me cringe, and I banished the memory to the far ends of my brain. Kole never discussed it, preferring to pretend it had never happened, and I'd been all too eager to comply. But if I'd pushed him to get treatment before now, would things be different? In some ways, was I just as guilty of the damage he now suffered?

That's it, I realized. While grief was a massive transport train that refused to leave me alone, guilt was the engine that drove it. First my conversation with Mom that convinced her to . . . make her choice, and then my allowing Kole to accompany me to Neuromen the night everything fell apart. The night Travers lost his wife and I nearly lost Dad and Kole. So much loss. Too much pain. But it wasn't grieving I needed now. The reminders came like tiny blades when I least expected them, tearing my heart into pieces from the inside. If I relented even the tiniest bit, allowing myself to crack, the pain would overcome me and I would shatter completely. I couldn't break apart when NORA needed me so badly.

The time would come, but it was not today.

I swallowed the lump in my throat and placed a hand on Travers's shoulder. "I'm so sorry about your wife. Losing a loved one, it . . . it changes everything."

My words were terribly inadequate, but my driver—no, my friend—seemed to understand. "Thank you. But we aren't here for me. Your father lies at the brink of death, your mother beyond it, and you've lost your brother in every sense of the word."

And maybe Kole soon too, I wanted to say, but that invisible rope had tightened itself around my throat. I nodded again.

"I have no advice for you," he continued, his own voice strained. "Once, I may have, but today . . . well, I think this is what your father would have done. When the living can't give you answers, perhaps the dead can." He handed me a stunner. "Just in case."

I looked past him to the statue of my dead mother. The hunk of metal held no answers for me today, but Travers looked at me with such pity, such pain, that I simply nodded and opened my door. Maybe he needed this as much as I did.

Stalking across the dying lawn meant watching the decline of my city in real-time. The park's clean sidewalks and carefully tended lawn had become overgrown in only a few short weeks. Across the field near the playground, a community of sleeping bags and haphazard tents extended along the entire far end of the sidewalk. I'd passed this a few weeks ago and seen people huddled around makeshift fire pits. But the tents and sleeping bags lay quiet now. I stepped softly so I wouldn't wake them.

Dad rarely mentioned the homeless except to say they made their own choices and he wouldn't interfere. But I'd always wondered about that. When given two choices, why would someone choose to live on the streets unless the cost of living in a warm home had become too high?

I reached the statue and halted, looking around once more. A deep sigh rose unbidden, and I felt a wide smile cross my face. For the first time in weeks, I was utterly alone. I liked the feeling more than I should. If I was meant to be NORA's leader, I would have to get used to guards following me around, cameras in my face, reporters asking what I ate for dinner, and politicians demanding favors. The past weeks of constant stress were only the beginning.

Gram rose to power at sixteen. I would be eighteen in a few weeks. Yet, somehow, I still felt like that little girl who tore the crust off her bread and wanted to wear the same dress every day. Even if I managed to defeat Alex, could I put my own brother in jail for the rest of his life? If I took the throne, could I banish Kole's friends for following their leader's orders? Would I spend the rest of my life pretending to be my grandmother?

Did I even want this?

Gram hadn't. I remembered her admission the day before my Declaration, the day I'd torn free of my family's expectations only to have them fall into my lap later.

Country over family. Country over self. Dad's creed, and certainly one he lived by. The distant, dismissive motto of a nonfunctional family I belonged to only by chance. Yet the biological family I'd sprung from didn't want me either.

I have a message from Legacy's mother. Chadd's words from last night. If only Kole hadn't driven him off. I would have been able to tell right away whether the guy lied or not. Wouldn't I? Or did my childlike hunger for belonging make me as vulnerable to manipulation as Kole claimed?

I sighed, turning to the statue once more. Mom would've hated it. It wasn't even a statue exactly—more like a piece of abstract art in the shape of a woman some artist had given Dad after her death, probably to launch his own fame. The artist's name was larger than Mom's on the plaque, after all. I wished her name weren't on it at all. Nothing about the stone so prominently placed in a public park reminded me of Mom other than the unveiling event I'd refused to attend but watched live from the privacy of my room. Stone made things permanent. Cold. Unfeeling. Mom wasn't any of those things.

It was pretty in its own way, I had to admit. I placed a hand on the lump extending skyward from her arched form, likely an arm. The artist had explained that Mom reached upward as if imploring the heavens for more knowledge, exhibiting the hunger that described her entire life. *Until the end*, I'd added in my mind, as had much of the country. Not that it mattered what they thought. It didn't matter what anyone thought, really. Solving the mystery of her death hadn't changed a thing. Mom would never come back.

"My biological mother may want to meet me," I told the statue.

The silver plating gleamed in the sunlight now, and I saw a distorted version of my face in its polished metal.

"I can ignore her. She abandoned me, after all. Might be nice to return the favor."

What would Mom have said had this happened in another lifetime? Would she have encouraged me to meet the woman or refuse to respond? Something told me my birth mother was a mystery Mom would have loved to solve, if only to settle the matter in her mind. She attacked every question with the scientific method. A meeting would mean new evidence that ultimately led to the conclusion that I was better off now. Happily ever after, close the book. The end.

But what if it meant the opposite? What if I wasn't really meant to lead NORA and my birth mother offered a different life?

Distant, muffled voices sounded across the field. Figures walked around now, whispering amongst themselves. Time to go. As hesitant as I felt earlier about being here, I didn't want to leave. I faced the statue once more, somehow feeling like this would be my last opportunity for answers.

"What would you do right now, Mom?" I whispered softly. "Dad is in a coma, Gram is sick, and the country is torn in half. Would you put your family first if it meant failing your duty to the country? Or would you hurt your family if it meant keeping NORA safe?"

My words rang hollow in my ears. I felt foolish. She'd already made that decision. She'd sacrificed everything, including her family. I'd find no answers here.

"Do you like it? 'Cause I don't."

I whirled to find a little boy standing behind the statue, staring at my mother's monument with a pinched frown. He couldn't be older than six. A smattering of freckles covered his nose and cheeks.

I pretended to examine the statue again, relieved he hadn't recognized me. "No, I don't like it at all."

"It doesn't even look like a person. A monster, maybe. One of those big gray ones."

I nodded solemnly. "The gray ones are the worst."

"Definitely." He gave me a sideways look. "Do they chase you too?"

I thought of my dreams over the past week. I had monsters to deal with, too, and they didn't leave when I awoke. "Yes."

The boy leaned forward and lowered his voice to a whisper. "I have a good hiding place. You can use it some-time, but you can't tell anyone." He pointed toward a fir tree whose lower branches extended so wide it looked like a ballerina with a flared skirt. "We could both fit under there."

I smiled at him. "Is that where you sleep?"

"No. That's where I hide when the monsters come." He gave the homeless community a sweeping glance. "You'd better hide because they'll be here soon. They always come when it gets light."

A quick look around revealed no alarmed parents or older siblings. Wasn't anyone concerned for the little boy who'd wandered from the safety of the group? "Is your mom or dad nearby?"

"My mom's dead. The monsters hurt my dad and made him sick. He's in the tent with the other sick ones, but don't worry. He won't be mad I showed you my hiding place."

I glanced across the field again, trying to make sense of his words. Monsters? I supposed Virgil's update could seem like a monstrous event. Kids processed things differently than adults. "How many are sick?"

"Three. Two more died yesterday, but they took them away."

I knelt to look the boy directly in the eyes. "Will you show me? I want to see if I can help your dad." Our hospital was already full, but surely we could fit three more patients. In the meantime, I'd have an assistant find a foster family to take the boy. I couldn't leave him here alone, hiding in trees from imaginary bad guys.

"Okay," he said after a moment and took off toward the tents at a run. I jogged to follow.

As he opened the tent flap, the heavy scent of unwashed bodies slammed into me. Two still forms filled the small tent. A smaller form lay between them, the girl's hair splayed across a rolled-up sweater serving as her pillow.

I frowned. Children didn't receive implants until age twelve. Could this be a different illness?

"That's my dad," the boy said, pointing to the man on the right. He had red hair identical to the boy's and a long, prominent nose that made his face look rectangular. His chest moved almost imperceptibly with each breath. I could tell by the shadows on his face and the sickly white pallor of his skin he wouldn't be with us much longer. A bright-red vertical scar crossed one side of his forehead as if someone had slashed him with a very precise and tiny blade.

I examined the other two with a sinking heart. They

both had the same scar in the same place. They looked as sickly as the father.

I turned slowly back to the boy, trying to put the pieces together. No matter how I tried, they didn't fit. Who would do such a thing and why? The only reason I could think of involved inserting an object under the skin, something flat and small . . .

Oh, fates.

Something about the size of a Rating screen.

"What are you waiting for?" the boy asked, still holding the tent open. "You said you would help them."

I took in a shaky breath, trying to keep my composure as the dread sunk in. "I need to go back to my transport and make a call. My friends will be here soon to help your dad. Would you like a better place to sleep tonight?"

The boy nodded, then stopped as if listening. His eyes went wide with panic. "They're here."

SIX

LEGACY

THE BOY BOLTED for the fir tree.

In confusion, I watched him go, then looked around the park to see an Enforcer patrol vehicle pulling into the parking lot. Odd. Alex had disbanded the Enforcers and replaced them with . . . *Oh, no.*

Six Firebrands dressed in dark-gray uniforms stepped out of the vehicle and strode across the lawn toward us.

Gray monsters.

I cursed and looked around for a place to hide. A man peeked out of his tent and motioned for me to enter. "Hurry!"

There wasn't time to consider. I ducked inside and stood as the man zipped the tent back up, surprised to find an entire family inside. They sat amongst a pile of blankets, looking terrified. Then the man unrolled part of the window flap to peek outside. When none of his family members moved, I stepped up to join him. Screams sounded from across the camp.

Whatever these soldiers wanted, it wasn't to check on the homeless people's welfare.

The Firebrands, four men and two women, stalked straight to the tent I'd stood outside just a minute before. They muttered amongst themselves as one ducked inside. A minute later, he emerged and said, "Two more to replace the ones from yesterday."

The Firebrands looked around, their stunners lifted. One shoved her way into a neighboring tent. Someone screamed, and then the flap opened and the woman came out, dragging a girl about my age. The girl's wailing cut off when the group of Firebrands lifted her to her feet, at least four stunners against her head. An assortment of curse words burst into my mind.

"A man this time, about forty-five," the Firebrand woman said.

Three of her colleagues headed for our tent.

The family behind me gasped, and the mother shushed the youngest with a finger to her lips. I reached for my stunner, feeling sick, then lowered my hand again. This weapon could help me take out one of them, maybe two. There would be no time for the third. Besides, the commotion would bring the others upon us in seconds. The Firebrands' surprise discovery of Legacy Hawking inside a homeless family's tent wouldn't stop anything, and my capture would mean certain victory for Alex and his Firebrands. I had to be smart about this.

The time for fighting will come.

The door flap opened. I turned my head away, hiding my face. It didn't muffle the sounds of soft weeping from the corner and the scuffle of a man trying to defend himself. A heavy sound meant they'd hit him with something and he'd fallen limply to the ground. The mother gasped. Then the sound of a body being dragged filled the tent.

A new anger sent my heart racing. How dare the Firebrands treat people this way? How dare Alex sit in the Copper Office, refusing to see the violence that kept him there, doing nothing about any of this?

As the group retreated, I hurried to secure the door flap and faced the man's family, my voice shaking with rage as I whispered, "What are they going to do with him?"

She shook her head quickly, as if not daring to speak. I looked out the window again, following the group back to the center of the tents and out of sight. I angled myself at the edge of the window but still couldn't see them. I didn't dare open the tent door with those armed Firebrands so close, not when it could put this family in even more danger.

"Lay them down," a sharp voice ordered. "And hold them properly this time, will you? The incision has to be precise."

Fates. Was this how Alex intended to switch NORA over to the Rating system, one by one in a dirty public park and starting with those who couldn't defend themselves? Or was this some kind of test?

I fingered the stunner in my pocket once again, trying to think. The world somehow seemed red and spotty, and all I wanted to do was burst out of this tent and start shooting. Something felt very wrong about all this. Those three unconscious forms in the tent had to be the missing link. Why would implantation make someone sick? Their incisions didn't look infected, yet all three lay near death. Gram hadn't mentioned anyone from her generation dying when the thin screen was placed. A new material, maybe? It had been nearly fifty years since we dropped the technology for good. Or so we thought.

The Firebrands talked quietly amongst themselves. I caught a word here and there. Something about a glue seal and testing procedures. The rest of the tent community hid in terrified silence. When the man grunted and there was a shuffling sound, it seemed much louder than it should have in the too-still morning air.

Please be done, I pled with the fates. Once the Firebrands left, I could tend to the victims. Maybe if we slid the screens back out, they wouldn't be affected like the others. I would take these people back to the safe house with me and protect them from this awful situation. I raised my eyebrows hopefully to the mother, but she just looked down and held her children even tighter, her expression pained.

She knew exactly what was happening, and it wasn't over yet.

"Uploading," the female Firebrand who'd dragged the teenage girl said. "It should take effect in three, two, one."

Uploading? That didn't sound like implantation. It sounded more like a brain-implant update. But why . . . ?

Then the screaming began.

The teenage girl's terrified wailing pierced the cool morning air, but it was the father's strained groaning that chilled my blood. It was the sound of incomprehensible pain, an agony that made this man's family tremble and weep.

I stood, the sudden rush of blood in my ears compounding my anger as I whipped out my stunner. Alone or not, I couldn't sit here and listen any longer.

I unzipped a portion of the tent, the sound muffled by the increasing screams. Then I aimed my stunner at the nearest Firebrand's back and pulled the trigger.

He arched his back and hit the ground.

I got in two more shots—another hit that took down one of the women and a wide miss—before the Firebrands realized what was happening. They scattered, weapons lifted, searching for the source of the shots and leaving their victims thrashing on the ground.

The sight stole my resolve and my breath all at once. In that moment, all I could see was Kole on all fours, his back arched in silent agony, his face contorted with a pain I would never be able to comprehend.

Footsteps pounded toward me, shaking me back to the present. I took down one more Firebrand but missed his chest, getting his thigh instead. He hit the ground hard and howled as the other three took cover again.

I had to draw them away from these people. Throwing the tent door open so hard the zipper broke, I dove through it and stumbled to keep my footing. Then I sprinted across the lawn toward my transport, hoping Travers was still there. I ducked just as a massive wave of wind swept past me. I then leaped behind Mom's statue just as a second struck. The metal reverberated, absorbing the impact with a strained, low protest. I peeked around the side and got off a few more shots, all of which went wide. Then I bolted again. Almost there.

The transport faced the street now, my door open and waiting. *Bless you, Travers.* For the second time in as many days, I dove into the open door and we were off.

I tossed the closing harness aside and gasped for air, turning around in my seat. The Firebrands had rerouted and were headed for their vehicle.

"Perhaps when this is over, you can explain what you were thinking," Travers growled.

"It wasn't my fault. They—"

"When this is over," he repeated quickly, snapping open a dashboard compartment. He retrieved what looked like a wheel, then slammed it into the dashboard amongst all the instruments. It clicked into place. He gripped it with one hand and flipped a switch with the other.

"Security code SREVART!" he shouted.

"Accepted," the transport said, and there was an audible shift in the engine. Travers grabbed the wheel with both hands and leaned forward. It was then I understood what was happening.

He'd just switched the transport to manual. I didn't even know it could do that.

"Did you install this feature?" I asked when I'd recovered my voice.

"Your father did. All the family vehicles have them. This one has a few extra surprises, however, things Malachi Hawking paid for but didn't know about." He paused. "*Doesn't* know about."

Our vehicle picked up speed, weaving around slower transports toward a side road. As we did, two other vehicles, both armored Enforcement transports, pulled in behind the first. They matched our speed easily. Too easily.

Travers groaned. Whatever override system our vehicles had, theirs obviously did too. No wonder they'd stolen Enforcer vehicles. With three of them chasing us, our chances weren't great.

"Those number screens they forced people to wear in Old NORA," I began, still finding my breath. "The Fire-brands were implanting the homeless. But they mentioned some kind of update. Were the original screens connected to a brain implant?"

Travers frowned. "I don't think so. Perhaps we should discuss it with your grandmother *after* we escape."

The not-so-subtle reminder of our circumstances brought me back to reality. Those Firebrands had to know who I was. By now, Alex would too. He would order every armored Enforcement transport in the city after us within minutes. I had only a stunner, a single transport, and a determined driver for protection. My only comfort was the fact that Alex didn't want me dead. He would order me arrested.

Wham!

The explosion of sound threw me backward and against the door.

I flung my arms out to catch myself, grunting as my head hit the back of Travers's seat. Then our momentum flung me against my own seat, entangling me in my empty harness. I pushed free and looked around in confusion, my ears ringing.

What had just happened?

Travers grabbed the wheel again, steering us back onto the road. Then he shot a horrified look behind us.

"What was that?" I shouted. My voice sounded muffled, as if coming from a distance. I couldn't understand Travers's reply. By the bewildered look on his face, I could tell he'd experienced the same thing I had. How was the transport holding together after an explosion like that?

I turned around to stare out the back window and then ducked down in my seat. One of the large vehicles had nearly caught up to us. A Firebrand hung out the window, hefting what looked like a massive stunner in both hands. He frowned at the top of the weapon as if reading some kind of gauge.

It was far too large to be a stunner. Maybe a stunner *cannon*. No wonder our transport had shaken like it was coming apart. We couldn't handle many more blasts like that.

I had so many questions. How long had those weapons existed? Did Dad know? Did the guard have access to those, or were they a Firebrand weapon? Were there others? How was I supposed to defeat an army with a few hand stunners when they had those? Most importantly, what was that weapon's weakness? Surely it took time to recharge before each shot, or the soldier would have launched another shot at us while I sat there, staring at him out the the—

Wham!

The vehicle shook violently once more, nearly launching us off the road again. I ducked and covered my ears, though it was too late to prevent the huge wave of pressure from hitting my eardrums. Travers managed to keep his seat this time, although he slid several inches forward and ducked his head at the impact. As I sat up, I noticed a long, spiderlike crack in the rear window.

" . . . down!" Travers shouted. The sound came in bursts of clarity, and I realized he was ordering me to stay on the floor. If the window broke, I'd be vulnerable to whatever that thing was. And then . . .

Fates. They weren't just trying to stop the transport.

They were trying to kill us.

"Hold on!" Travers shouted, his voice stronger than before. I barely had time to duck before we launched sideways into an alley, clipping the side of a building and knocking a side mirror clean off.

The transport just behind us missed the turn, but the other two followed.

Travers's jaw clenched, and both hands tightened on the wheel. The alley was dark and narrow. If they managed to halt our transport, we wouldn't even be able to open the door to escape.

Then I'll have to make sure they don't stop us.

I whipped the stunner from my pocket and let my finger hesitate over the switch. Stun mode wasn't likely to make much of a difference with an armored vehicle protecting those soldiers. Clearly, these guys meant for Travers and me to die today. This was no time for hesitation. I flipped it to fatal mode, opened the side window, and sent off a couple of quick shots. But nothing happened.

Our vehicle rocked with another impact, shards of glass flying in my direction. I ducked again and threw my arms over my head.

Travers swore from the front seat. "Are you all right?"

I carefully lifted my face, finding my hair buried in glass, and shook it off. Then I brushed away any remaining glass and glanced back. The rear window was completely blown out.

One more shot and we were goners.

I lifted the stun gun once more and shot at the driver. Nothing, not even the sound of ricocheting. The Firebrand shooting the stun cannon retreated inside. Only one kind of shot would stop that thing, and that shot required the best aim of my life.

I had to take out that Firebrand.

It felt like an eternity before he appeared at the side window again, lining us up along the barrel of the stun cannon. I growled in frustration. Not much of his face showed, and the road was bumpy, but I wouldn't have another chance. I aimed and yanked on the trigger.

An explosion unlike any of the others ripped the air apart, throwing me across the vehicle. I gritted my teeth as pain sliced through my hands, arms, and face.

The transport flew forward just as Travers turned onto a side road, the momentum throwing us toward another transport headed in the opposite direction. I caught a glimpse of the terrified man in the front seat. His vehicle must have deployed its emergency halting mechanism because we missed him by centimeters.

Travers gained control of the transport once more, his face drained of color. I shook myself free of glass again, cursing at the tiny bleeding cuts on my palms, and turned back toward the rear window only to see the other transport disappear behind us. It had smashed against the wall of a clothing store, black smoke curling up from the engine. Just then, the second Enforcer vehicle rammed into its backside, flinging the first into the street. A third swung wide to avoid hitting it.

I stared at the stunner in my hand. How . . . ?

Then understanding dawned. I'd missed the gunner, but he'd pulled his trigger at the same time. Stunners used sound waves to incapacitate a target. The two waves, though very different in force, had collided midair and caused some kind of explosion that threw them off course.

"Yes! You did it, Miss Hawking!" Travers shouted. Even as he finished, his grin faded and his jaw clenched. I whirled around to find that the third vehicle had abandoned the others and now plunged headlong after us.

"Go, go, go!" I yelled, watching through the space where the back window had been. An unmistakable shadow, black and heavy, sat in the front passenger's arms. Another stun cannon.

My throat grew so tight I could barely breathe. I'd been lucky the first time. There was no way I could repeat it.

"See if you can lose them," I shouted at Travers, aiming my stunner at their vehicle and releasing a couple of quick shots at their windshield. Nothing. Not even a crack, and they'd already begun to close the distance between us.

We needed a plan. If only we had something stronger to shoot at that windshield—or perhaps *throw* at it.

I gave my seat a sideways look. Dad had commissioned it after purchasing the vehicle, having fitted it specifically to the shape of my body. What else had he added for extra protection? I reached beneath the seat and began to fumble with one of the latches.

"What are you doing?" Travers asked.

"Don't worry about it. Just keep them from shooting at us."

"How am I supposed to do that?"

I grunted, throwing my weight behind the last latch. "Evasive maneuvering? I don't know. You're the one who reads all the books."

"Romances," he muttered. "I read romances." But he gritted his teeth and yanked the wheel sideways, sending me scrambling to secure myself so I didn't slide into the piles of glass again. Just as he straightened out, a giant whoosh blew past us. We'd barely missed that one.

"Perfect!" I shouted. "Now, pretend we're in a romance novel and the bad guy is after your busty blonde heroine. What would you do?"

"I don't think that comparison quite works here, Miss Hawking."

The vehicle straightened out just in time for another sharp turn to the left. I braced the now-loose seat against my body, although it still tilted toward Travers. I caught it with my leg before it could tumble into the front, then lowered it to the ground beside me. It was heavier than I imagined. Lined with some kind of metal, perhaps.

Thanks, Dad.

Travers swore again and swerved. This time the shot caught us halfway. Without the back window in place, the whoosh was much stronger. The wave of air nearly picked up the vehicle and threw us as strongly as the interference wave had earlier.

"The transport can't take another one of those," Travers called out. "Did you say you had some kind of brilliant plan?"

"No. A risky plan will have to do. Can you let them get closer?"

"*Closer?*"

"Just trust me." Although I didn't even trust myself. If this didn't work, I could very well be sentencing us both to death. The soldiers would drag our bodies back to Alex, and the Copper Office would be his forever. Dad wouldn't last long, nor Gram, and Kole would . . .

No.

We would *not* lose this battle today. The thought thrust itself upon my mind as forcefully as anything, startling me with the intensity of it.

Travers slowed the transport, its high-pitched whining lowering in pitch by the second. Good. Let them think the battery had taken a hit and we'd soon be theirs. Maybe it meant they would hold off on the stun cannon for a few seconds. That was all I needed. Just a few seconds . . .

The sound of cheering behind us meant they were much closer than before. Was it close enough? Did I dare lift my head to find out, or would they blast it off at the first opportunity?

The electric whining of their engine rose in pitch as it drew closer and closer.

Now.

I lifted the seat in front of me, angled it, and heaved it through the back with a mighty yell.

Their driver tried to swerve, but he had little time. The seat hit the street, bounced, and smashed through his windshield. The vehicle lurched to one side and smashed into a light pole, which teetered, paused, and then plunged to the ground.

Travers turned us down the next street, and the scene disappeared behind us.

SEVEN

KOLE

Thanks to my self-imposed spying missions, I knew exactly where Dane's headquarters stood.

My uncle no longer used his home. Ever since Alex's order to disband the Enforcers who didn't support him, they'd occupied the old Enforcer building around the corner from the Block. One of those old-fashioned, gray, two-story buildings, the structure looked like something once owned by the fire team. I avoided the front door and its fingerprint lock, instead swinging around to the side. This door had an implant-code lock—the type that clicked open only when you had brain-implant authorization. Firebrands were as cocky as Enforcers were paranoid. They didn't expect to be attacked in their stronghold. Surely they'd left something unlocked.

Ignoring the pounding in my skull and pain slicing through my rib cage with every breath, I carefully examined every window until I found an open one in back, voices floating through from inside.

I heaved it open and slid inside in a single movement, muting my screaming muscles to a dull buzz.

There was a crash as someone jumped to their feet behind a desk. Zenn, Not Dane. He'd stopped shaving since I saw him last, and the dark scruff he now sported on his chin met with thick sideburns in front of his wide ears. In another lifetime, he'd been one of my best friends.

"Where is he?" I roared.

"K-Kole," Zenn sputtered, grabbing the closest object on the desk. A pen. He lifted it but made no move toward me. "You can't just break in like you belong here." He usually hid his accent better. I'd truly startled him.

"If I belonged, I wouldn't be breaking in. Where is Dane?"

"He isn't here, I swear. Why do you look like you just walked through a campfire?"

"Very funny." Except he looked genuinely confused. Baffled. Concerned, even. "You really don't know?"

His thick, black eyebrows drew together in confusion. "Know what? That you're sleeping in chimneys now? Why the fates would I know where you've been? You're the one who abandoned us and ran off with some doomed heiress."

So that was Dane's dialogue. He'd conveniently left out the hospital attack where he killed my mom and chased me off. And Legacy was no doomed heiress. She was the future leader of NORA. I'd make sure of it.

"Dane tried to kill me," I snapped. "Set my building on fire and killed a dozen innocent people."

He looked genuinely stunned. "I didn't know, man. I'm really sorry." He glanced at the window I'd just entered and took a step back as I approached. "But are you sure it was us? I mean, we didn't light anything up last night. Dane isn't even in town. He went to—went somewhere." There was a note of defensiveness in his tone.

Some of the anger drained from my chest like a doused

flame. At least Zenn knew where Dane was. "So Dane had some other coward set the fire. Big deal."

"You really think he'd let someone else kill you? He's been muttering about strangling you for weeks. If he knew you were here right now, after all our searching, he'd . . ." He clamped his mouth shut. "You don't have much time left, man. If I were you, I'd turn around and disappear."

So Dane had scoured the city, wanting me dead. It meant my decision to live away from Legacy had been the right one. "Not until you tell me where Dane went."

"You know I can't talk."

It was then I noticed his hand reach into the desk drawer. I leaped over the desk and slammed him against the wall, pinning him there. "Tell me where he is, Zenn."

My former friend's eyes narrowed as he struggled against my arms. The movement tore at my sore ribs, stoking the flames consuming me from the inside. Any injuries I bore now were preferable to what could have happened. What Dane had intended to happen.

"I swore the oath," Zenn snapped, shoving my arms away. "So did you."

"We swore to bring freedom to the city, not terror. Don't pretend the Firebrands didn't start those other fires too. I know you did."

"We had our orders," he admitted. "But we always clear the building first. If people died, it wasn't us. And if Dane wants you dead, he will succeed. All Firebrand traitors eventually vanish. Seems like you'd know that better than anyone, Mason." Zenn shoved me backward, forcing me to stumble and hit the desk with my lower back. It sent pain screaming through my rib cage. I gritted my teeth to hide a grunt. The last thing I needed was for Zenn to know my current state.

"Here's a thought," I said, rising to my full height to glare down upon my former friend. "Maybe Firebrands shouldn't be killing anyone."

He gave an incredulous snort. "I don't know what you thought we were doing here, but it wasn't making pretty speeches about a world full of rainbows. This is the real world."

"Well, maybe I've seen both sides and realized I was on the wrong one. I'll give you five seconds to tell me where Dane is, or I'll send your nose through your brain. Five . . . four . . ."

He smirked. "Wrong side, huh?"

"Three . . . two . . ."

His arm jerked upward, and a stunner appeared in my face. He'd managed to grab it after all.

I shoved the barrel aside just as he pulled the trigger. A portion of the blast caught me in the shoulder, sending me tumbling across the desk and to the floor. I hit hard and rolled a few feet toward the open window. A pained gasp escaped my throat as the room blurred around me, going gray at the edges.

Don't black out. Don't black out.

Zenn opened another drawer, removed a pair of cuffs, and stepped around the desk. He meant to keep me here till Dane returned.

He was about to be very disappointed.

My legs shot out as he approached, my foot connecting with his shin. He howled and dropped the cuffs as he leveled the stunner at my chest. I rolled out of the way just as another blast hit the floor. Then I launched to my feet and swung a fist to his face. It connected just as he turned.

Now he was the one who flew across the desk, toppling

his chair. I stepped around both to find him lying there, looking dazed.

"Tell me where he went!" I shouted. My headache flared, causing spots in my vision.

"No," he managed.

I threw my rage into a single kick to the temple. His head snapped sideways, and he toppled to the ground.

Footsteps sounded behind me. I turned in time to see a figure rushing me from the doorway. He slammed me against the desk. My head hit the surface, making the already-blurry room float oddly. I fought the darkness rushing in as I slid to the floor, my breath wheezing alarmingly. Every centimeter of my body ached now—from my scraped fingers to my torn feet and burned face. I imagined what it would feel like to let my head fall to the side, to give in and let the blackness take me. Zenn was right. If Dane wanted me dead, I couldn't escape him forever. Better to face death sooner than later.

No, a little voice inside protested. It was the Kole Mason who'd grown up in the Shadows, doing whatever it took to survive. The boy who'd spent his childhood cowering under his covers, afraid to breathe in case his drunk father heard him and remembered he existed. The boy who'd dug in dumpsters for his dinner countless times. The Kole Mason who had climbed down a building just last night to survive. If that Kole disappeared, who would be left to face Dane? I couldn't let Legacy do it alone.

The newcomer closed in again, wearing a smile that said he knew I was beaten. When he got close enough, I threw a kick to his stomach that sent him stumbling toward the door, where another newcomer emerged. I cursed. The longer I took to end this, the less chance I had of getting out of here.

I scooped the stunner from where Zenn had dropped it,

yanked him up from the floor, and held him like a dummy. Then I placed the stunner to his head and flipped it to fatal mode, watching the guy's eyes widen at the audible click. "Tell me where my uncle is, *right now*."

The two halted their approach, their eyes flicking from the weapon to Zenn.

"I've killed before," I told Zenn. "I'll do it again. Tell me!"

He shook his head ever so slightly and moaned. Hot, slick blood coated my hands, and I realized it came from his head. *Must have hit the desk on his way down.* Guilt cooled my anger, bringing everything into sharp focus. Me against three Firebrands with more on the way, and I'd just threatened a good friend's life. Zenn slumped against my arms, half conscious.

What demented part of my brain had chosen this plan?

The newcomer's irises turned a light-pink color and began to flick around. The IM-NET, probably composing some kind of message to Dane. Within seconds, my uncle would know I was here. I had to get out now.

One of the guys sprinted out the door, probably to get a weapon. I fired but missed. While I was distracted, the other lunged toward me.

I swung the stunner at him and took the shot, hitting him dead-on. He jerked in midair and slid to the floor near my feet, falling still at last.

Then I lowered Zenn to the ground and straightened, breathing hard. I'd have to find Dane some other way. I'd be long gone before these two came to their senses.

Wait.

I looked closer at the guy on the floor. His chest wasn't moving, and he stared sightlessly at the ceiling. Stunned people didn't stare like that.

Pain gripped me as I stared at the stunner.

Fatal mode.

I'd killed him.

"You're just like your dad," Zenn whispered from the floor. "A monster."

Shouts sounded from upstairs. I knew I should run, but my earlier rage had dissipated, taking my adrenaline with it. I couldn't tear my eyes away from the Firebrand on the floor, his shirt exposing the corner of a tattoo identical to mine. He looked to be around the same age. In another life, it could have been me.

I tossed the stunner across the room, hearing it hit the wall with a satisfying crack, then leaped out the window and into the street beyond.

EIGHT

LEGACY

"It's no use arguing about a course that has already been taken," Travers said in his calmest voice, likely trying to diffuse the tension in the living room. "What matters is what we learn from the events of the morning."

Everyone remained seated, even our three guests, though there were a lot of frowns. Gram sat in a high-backed, floral-patterned chair, looking every bit the regal ex-leader she was. She wore no less than three sweaters and a single blanket over her lap. At Gram's insistence, Physician Redd had remained after a quick precautionary examination of me and Travers, ignoring my protests the entire time. He had more important things to worry about than a few cuts from the glass and my sore neck.

The only two remaining members of Dad's cabinet looked at each other, silent communication passing between them. Chairman Barber, a man with a rapidly receding hairline and bulbous head that sat right upon his shoulders, seemed incapable of smiling as always. Chairwoman Marium, a red-haired woman with pale skin and a black hairpin, perched next to him with perfect posture and a scathingly judgmental expression, her shoes resting daintily on the floor.

Six people. The fate of NORA rested on the shoulders of the six people in this room, and we'd spent most of the last hour arguing instead of accomplishing anything.

Marium glared narrowly at Travers. "And what did we learn, driver? That our honored leader's recklessness endangered her life while you sat back and watched?"

Travers's face went red. "Our traveling the city alone during the day was a mistake, as I've said several times already. It won't happen again."

I jumped in before the argument could begin anew. Recklessness, indeed. If I were a man, it would have been deemed bravery. How did Dad handle such meetings without losing his ever-loving mind? "We know the Firebrands are implanting the homeless community, maybe experimenting on them. We don't have to know why in order to help them. I've already sent armed guards to bring them to safety, and I won't apologize for that. It was the right thing to do."

"We don't know that implantation was the cause of that mysterious illness," Councilman Barber said. "They could be contagious and infect everyone else. Homeless people aren't exactly known for their hygiene, after all."

I found myself on my feet, fists balled. "If you don't care about the people we're trying to protect, I'm not sure you should be here at all."

The councilman looked unfazed. "I've been a councilman since before your birth, Your Honor. Our people are only as safe as the laws that govern us. All I'm saying is that you should have consulted with the council before putting us in additional danger by adding . . . those people."

"Those people won't be the only homeless ones if we

don't act quickly. We can't afford to waste time arguing over every single thing."

"And I say we can't afford to make dangerous mistakes. You're lucky to be alive right now, young Miss Hawking."

I caught Gram's eye and detected a hint of warning. I bit back my next retort and calmed my breathing, trying to look unaffected. "You will address me with the appropriate title, Councilman."

The man looked startled for the first time. He glanced around, then sank into his chair. "My apologies, Your Honor."

I turned back to Physician Redd. "You were saying?"

Our family physician clutched his hands in front of him, looking very out of place. He probably had a thousand things to do right now, yet he was stuck in a meeting that went in circles. "My understanding is that implant screens cannot cause pain."

"Except that's not entirely true," Gram interrupted. "It's not that the screens can't cause harm. It's that they can't do it alone."

The room went silent. "What do you mean?" I asked.

Gram frowned. "In our day, we had techbands and implants. If you tried to remove one, it triggered what we called "punishment mode." Somehow, the two were connected. Maybe that's what the Firebrands are trying to do—discourage people from trying to remove their implants. Assuming we ever figure out how to do it without killing the patient, that is."

"But why?" I asked. "People are disillusioned with their implants after what Virgil did. I don't see how forcing everyone to keep them helps Alex's cause. If anything, it will make the country angrier with him."

"He hasn't seemed all that concerned about his public image so far," Travers muttered.

I had to agree. Alex's allocation of medical care to his own followers and rejection of everyone else had sent a huge wave of supporters my way. Then he'd made an announcement about a Rating System committee examining the possibility of reinstating the old system. The country-wide riots began the next day. Hurting those who tried to remove their implants would only shorten his reign. Sooner or later, the people would rise up against him, with or without my help.

"They want us to have both the brain implant and the screen, then," Gram said. "That's where the control comes in. They must have been testing punishment mode on those poor dears, and now we know why. Nobody will miss those who don't have steady work. I agree with Legacy's decision to bring them in. When will we know they've made it safely?"

I nearly sighed with relief. "Foster will send word when it's done." I could only hope the rescue had gone smoothly. If Alex had sent all his Firebrands to that park to protect his little experiment, we were likely in for some losses. I couldn't think about that right now.

"I'll see if I can get an update," Travers said, sending a glare in the councilman's direction before striding out of the room.

"If you'll excuse me as well," Physician Redd said. "If we have more patients coming, I'll need to notify my assistants. I'd like to examine them the moment they arrive." He inclined his head toward me and followed Travers.

Councilwoman Marium and Councilman Barber exchanged an impatient look. They had no such excuse to leave, much as I wished for one. I wanted to dismiss everyone and do things my way, but that wasn't how this worked. If I intended to hold on to this position for any length of time, I'd have to get used to these pointless meetings.

I cleared my throat and continued. "If the Firebrands really are testing, that means Alex plans to launch the Rating system soon. We need to encourage people to resist. Even Alex's supporters won't stand behind someone who wants to hurt his citizens." I grimaced when I thought of the man and girl from earlier and the agony in their expressions. "This could turn the tide for us." It would also make taking over the Copper Office much easier when General Knox arrived with her soldiers, but my cabinet didn't know about that plan yet. I was glad I hadn't told them now. We would have spent the past few weeks arguing about my plan and still be right where we were now.

"If we had access," Councilwoman Marium said, "we could hack into the IM-NET and send out a message. But unfortunately, Alex has seized all relay stations except Neuromen, which you dealt with yourself, Your Honor, if I recall." Her eyes were sharp and accusing.

Gram gave a low growl from her perch across the room, but I jumped in before she could defend me. "I won't apologize for that either. We saved hundreds of lives."

The councilwoman leaned forward. "I don't know if I would call lying on a hospital bed in a coma being saved. Besides, copycats have set fires all over the city in retaliation. It's a miracle we haven't lost hundreds more."

"Those are no copycats," Gram snapped. "Those are Firebloods . . . Firebrands? The fire people act under my grandson Alex's direction. You can't blame any of that on Legacy."

"The point is," I said, staring down the councilwoman

and councilman, "Alex controls the flow of information right now. People believe what they're told. If we take just one station, we can hack into the system and get our message out." I rose to my feet again and began to pace the ornate rug covering the floor. "Is there a remote location with fewer guards?"

"Alex has increased security at every location," Councilwoman Marium said, looking sufficiently chastened. "We'd take huge losses in the attempt."

"Then we use the army Her Honor has been gathering all this time," Councilman Barber said evenly. "That's what they're for, is it not?"

I gritted my teeth and halted in front of my chair. "They came to us for help. I don't intend to send them into battle unless we have to."

"So your grand plan is to stare down the bad guys with the power of our righteous cause behind you and nothing else," he said. "That sounds like a disaster."

Councilwoman Marium covered her face with her manicured hands and groaned. "Please tell me we have a plan, Your Honor. Despite what it seems, we're on your side. It would help if you explained what we're doing here."

I took a long breath and exhaled forcefully. Everyone watched me expectantly, even Gram, who pressed her lips together worriedly. They were right. My cabinet deserved to know that much.

"I had a different army in mind," I began. "General Knox's soldiers. She's had dinner with my family many times, and we've grown close. She always joked I would have been a better general than leader of NORA. I think she'll side with me rather than Alex."

"So we just wait, then?" Barber shot back. "Wait and place our hopes in the lap of a general who obviously doesn't care that her country is falling apart? She's been at the border for over two years now."

Marium looked stricken, as if she agreed but didn't want to voice the words.

Gram shook her head. "Legacy may be right about the general. I don't know the woman very well. What I do know is that Alex will find us no matter what, so we may as well look at all our options. If getting the word out means knocking on doors and talking to people one-on-one, so be it. I've certainly had to do that before."

Barber's nose twitched, and I realized he hid a smile. "Forgive me, Your Honorable Treena Hawking, but times have changed. It would take years to reach everyone that way."

"And it will take forever for the Copper Office to fall into our lap because it won't happen," Gram snapped.

"We all agree on one thing," I interrupted. "There isn't much time. Physician Redd is doing what he can, but I don't know if we'll be able to safely remove implants anytime soon. Millian's lab has made huge strides in studying how implants work with the brain. If she succeeds, we won't have to remove them at all. Maybe we can permanently disconnect them rather than temporarily disable them. Then nobody can use them against us, Rating screens or not. But that will take time too. So we need to send a message out somehow. If we can do it in a public way, all the better."

The group fell silent again.

A full minute passed before Barber spoke up. "I admire your vision, Your Honor, but something so public would bring the Firebrands upon us in minutes. Secrecy would surely be the better course."

"I agree," Marium said.

"I disagree," Gram said.

Then the room filled with chatter again, everyone expressing their opinion and talking over each other. I could barely pick out one voice over another. Even Gram waved her bony arm in a dramatic fashion, facing down Barber while Marium leaped to his defense.

I plopped down into my chair again, feeling the effects of the morning and another sleepless night finally hit me. I wanted to shout for everyone to stop questioning my every move and leave me alone, but I saw their drawn expressions and the redness in their eyes. I wasn't the only person who cared about NORA, and I couldn't blame them for feeling as helpless as I did.

The problem with attending school rather than going to the office with Dad over the past few years was that I had no training in these matters. I'd sat in few meetings, collected few interpersonal skills, and argued no points whatsoever. Alex had more experience with all those things. His mind had always been in the right place, even if his heart wasn't.

The deep yearning that grew inside me felt like a black hole in my gut. *Dad.* He should have been here. He would have quieted everyone and guided the discussion in a more purposeful direction.

"Excuse me," Foster said, tapping me on the shoulder. I hadn't seen him enter.

I perked up. *Finally.* "You have news? The homeless community—are they safe? Are you seeing to their needs? Was there fighting? Are the sick—"

"They're fine," Foster said curtly, then realized he'd just interrupted me. "Uh, I'm sorry, Your Honor. Yes, we were able to rescue nearly all the community. Everyone except the implanted individuals, who were all missing. Witnesses say the Firebrands returned and took them away."

I thought of that little boy, now without either of his parents, and felt a lump in my throat. "You made sure they weren't followed to the warehouse?"

"Yes." He swallowed. For the first time, I noticed the paleness of his face. "Actually, Your Honor, that isn't why I'm here. You've received a message via one of our IM-NET readers. They managed to find some paper and copy it down for you. The contact said it came from the border." He held out the note.

My heart stuttered. I slowly reached up, pinching the folded paper between my fingers. It looked as if it had been torn from an old-fashioned book, one edge uneven, the page number 239 centered at the bottom of one side. Someone had glued it closed.

The room quieted once again, all eyes upon my hands. Foster retreated to the doorway but lingered, clearly hoping to learn what the message said before being dismissed.

"Finally," Gram breathed with relief.

I tore the secured edge free, then opened it and scanned its contents for the words I desperately needed to hear. The message was short and to the point.

"Well?" Gram asked. The others watched my face for any sign of good news.

I read the letter once, then twice, hoping its contents would change the second time. My insides deflated, everything that held me up to this point receding like draining water.

"General Knox can't help," I said, unable to keep the defeat from my voice. "Says her troops are needed at the border and can't be spared."

A somberness descended upon us. Even Gram's shoulders visibly sagged, and she slumped back against the chair, looking as exhausted as I felt.

I refolded the message and shoved it into my pocket. I knew exactly what this meant. General Knox had pledged an oath to Dad, not me or Alex. She'd wait until Dad recovered and took power again or the succession war resolved itself. I tried to sound unaffected, but I couldn't hide the bitterness in my voice. "Better she remain neutral than join Alex's side. With the Firebrands and military on his side, we'd be defeated in weeks."

Barber spoke up. "We may yet, I'm afraid. There's one thing you haven't considered, Your Honor. Those Firebrands meant to kill you. If they operate under your brother's command, we all have reason to fear. Our next actions may mean life or death for the entire group."

"I agree," Millian said, appearing in the entryway next to Foster. The two looked each other up and down, and Foster's face turned bright red. Millian gave him a quizzical look before striding inside, then turned to stand in front of the fireplace like an actress on stage. "You know the funny thing? Nobody ever thinks about inviting the scientist."

I grinned sheepishly. She was right. It hadn't occurred to me. "We were just discussing how to send a message to the general public without hacking the IM-NET."

Millian shrugged. "Easy. Interrupt a live broadcast. Reporters travel light since they have to get there in a hurry, so they don't bring guards with them. Just a producer and a cameraperson or two. If we can *persuade* a reporter to let us say our piece, we'd have at least a few seconds to get our message out before somebody cuts us off."

"That's ridiculous—" Councilwoman Marium began.

"No, wait," Gram said. "It's not a bad idea. Every time the arsonists act, reporters rush to the scene. If we prepare a statement and then stake out the firehouse, that could work."

"Or we send a team to follow a reporter around," Millian said. "Then we hijack their broadcast and say what we need to say. Legacy, you can write something convincing. Gram can polish it up, and Kole can help deliver it. He's one of the most recognizable faces among us, and those from the Shadows respect him. Assuming he's feeling up to it after last night." She looked around. "He's okay, right? I saw his building. Or what's left of it, I guess."

My lungs stopped functioning. "What?" I squeaked.

"The fire last night. You didn't hear?"

Dread filled my limbs until I could barely sit up straight. Wind roared in my ears. This couldn't be happening. "No." *No, no, no.*

"Sixteen dead," the councilwoman said. "They're still identifying the remains. I'm not familiar with this Kole person. Shall I check the reports?"

I barely heard her. My legs felt weirdly connected to the floor and wouldn't respond to my commands. My throat and my stomach felt tangled, their positions all wrong, and the room faded in and out.

Had Kole made it out, he would have come straight here. I knew it with everything in me. Something had to be very wrong.

Fire.

Sixteen dead.

Not Kole, not like this. We were supposed to have time . .
.

I felt a sob rise up from deep within, felt the torrent reach the surface. I was breaking apart here and now, on a fancy rug in a stranger's house in an unfamiliar part of town. I wanted my room, my house, my family. I wanted Kole here with me.

And then Millian was there, easing my arm around her shoulder, forcing me to lean into her.

"I'm taking Her Honor to her room," she called to the others, easing me toward the exit as Foster scrambled to hold the door.

Then she whispered into my ear. "There were a few injured taken to the city hospital. I'll track him down and bring him home, okay? But first, I'll end this awful meeting of yours. Don't worry. I know how to motivate the stuffy ones." She wrinkled her nose and shoved me toward the stairs.

My legs moved obediently, climbing the steps like I had dozens of times before, taking me to my bedroom in some kind of trance. I'd felt this way once before—the day Dad came to my school and told me about Mom. The day my life shattered, spilling sharp pieces all over me like the broken glass from the transport this morning. My palms still stung from the tiny shards, brilliant and sharp, a constant reminder of pain. Also like Mom.

I collapsed onto my bed and stared at the ceiling for a very long time.

NINE

KOLE

I was *not* my father.

A swift kick to the wall of a brick building sent a stabbing pain through my rib cage. I swore and continued walking, ignoring the lady next to me on the sidewalk as she looked me up and down, taking in the caked-on soot and dirt. Let her stare. Let her wonder about the dirty guy stalking the streets of the Shadows, cursing and kicking things. Maybe she would stay in the rich part of town where she belonged and leave me the fates alone.

Zenn was wrong about me. Dad hadn't concerned himself—No, wait. Not Dad. That term meant things I never got as a child. It meant playing catch in the backyard. It meant bedtime stories and tousling a kid's hair, asking how school was. It meant secret kisses between parents in the kitchen when they thought they were alone. It meant lectures and encouragement and caring.

My sperm-donor father was none of those things, and he'd only ever had two goals: power and alcohol. His Firebrand "meetings" offered heavy doses of both. Some of my earliest memories involved Dad with his friends, piles of forgotten playing cards scattered across the table; heavy belching, drunken laughter, and loud banging as a chair flew across the room or somebody collapsed and began to snore. He surrounded himself with people like him, both frustrated at their lack of progress but also determined to keep things precisely as they stood—because there, he had power. There, he ruled over his household and friends in his anger.

He lived at the bottom of a well, preferring the darkness of solidarity to the possibility of light and solitude.

It was that darkness I grew up in, a weed finding light reflected off several other surfaces, absorbing what remained when everyone else got what they needed. It was that darkness that had bred in me a hatred for everything light and unattainable and different and *Hawking*. I sat at my father's feet, listening to him swear oaths he would never fulfill and call for assassinations that would never come to pass.

Except now, plenty of people were dying, most of them better off than we ever were. My father would have been happy to see it.

I wasn't that way anymore. Legacy Hawking had become my redemption, my perspective, my enlightenment. But what did that matter if the world around me stayed exactly the same? At least the original Firebrands dared to dream, to reach higher and demand better. I'd switched sides and abandoned everything my family and I ever stood for. Some part of me, deep down, still hoped Dane and Alex would succeed in reinstating the Rating System and keep Legacy from the throne. Then we could be together in peace. No titles. No expectations. Just us.

I didn't belong in the Hawking mansion, and everyone knew it.

I reached an intersection and waited for the train to race by, blinking ash from my eyes. Time for a shower, but where? My old room at Dane's wasn't an option. I didn't dare visit Legacy at her home, especially now that every Firebrand in the city would be looking for me. I took a deep breath and winced at the pain in my chest, a new horror rising within. I'd marched into Firebrands HQ without a weapon and managed to escape.

What was I thinking?

All I remembered of my sprint across town at dawn was blind anger searching for a place to land. Wanting revenge more than life itself. Then there was the fear on Zenn's face as my fist connected, my roar as I tried to intimidate him, my finger on the trigger. The body on the floor. It was a scene I'd witnessed many times as a child but always at the hands of my father, never my own.

"I killed him to save Mom," I muttered as I followed the uneven sidewalk of the Shadows. Something deep inside released at the words, something that had spent far too long curled up like a weeping child, awaiting escape. My father killed to keep his power. Dane killed to earn his own. I had killed as a defense, a mercy. It wasn't the same thing.

But today's killing—what had that been?

A train rattled in the distance, speeding past our undesirable neighborhood. The next stop would be at least two kilometers away, on the edge of the suburbs. I had no intention of climbing aboard, not after what I'd just done. Every Firebrand in the city would be looking for me now.

"I'm not a bad person," I told the train, the lie echoing in the empty air. Good people didn't attack and threaten people they cared about. Good people wrapped a sheet around a stranger's waist to help them down a building just before they perished. Good people didn't put others at risk while they slept in their beds, oblivious.

Fates. All those people in my building.

I wanted Dane to take the blame so I didn't have to carry it any longer. But Zenn made a good point. The Firebrands cleared their buildings of occupants before striking the match. What if this hadn't been Dane at all? What if that Chadd guy had been the bigger threat all along? He could have been trying to rid the world of me to gain easier access to her. Or he could have returned, assumed Legacy was still inside, and tried to remove her for good. Worry spiked inside me. Time to warn her.

My feet slowed as I passed the old church, now a NORA museum. I hadn't gone in since the transformation. I preferred to remember it as it once stood—rows of hard benches, a wide aisle, architecture that seemed to extend into the sky itself. Mom and I would sit in the back row so we could escape the moment services ended. I couldn't remember a thing about those, but I recalled the large stained-glass window depicting a forest with perfect clarity. Not much remained of it now.

I craned my head, looking up at it. The museum had covered the bottom half with plywood and left the rest. All that remained were the tops of the tall trees and a blue sky, the tiny figures of people beneath them lost forever to history. I couldn't even remember who they were.

As a child, I'd tried to re-create the window with paper. It was painstaking work, requiring multiple colors and an old pair of scissors that didn't fit my hand and kept coming apart. I imagined the artist painting and cutting the glass, then carefully placing it. Nobody would have shouted at him for ruining that glass. He'd taken pieces of something mediocre and created something beautiful.

I felt like a random assortment of glass pieces right about now. Pieces of my father, my mother, Dane, Zenn, the Shadows, my job, and a hundred other things. I would be the one to turn ugly to beautiful. Me, the artist of my own life.

It sounded nice except for one problem—I'd never been good at art.

In the distance, a familiar figure stepped into the street and began to cross it.

I gaped, realized I was gaping, and ducked around the corner, breathing hard. Then I forced myself to chuckle. I saw enemies everywhere these days. My imagination was running wild after such a traumatic night and long morning. That couldn't possibly have been my prime suspect. I needed some food, a shower, pain meds, and a soft place to land for a few hours before my brain would function properly.

I put too much weight against the building, placing pressure on my rib cage. I gasped and gritted my teeth.

Okay, and maybe an ice pack or two.

When I'd finished convincing myself, I peered around the corner once again and blinked a few times. The man who looked like Chadd strode toward a brunette standing outside a worn-down transport repair shop now, a hat pulled low over his face. His bad posture and slender form looked strikingly familiar, but hundreds of guys could fit that description. The woman looked to be my mother's age or slightly younger. She looked familiar, too, but I couldn't place her.

I hesitated, wishing I'd grabbed that Firebrand stunner at HQ instead of throwing it. But I had to know—for Legacy's sake, if not my own.

The hard part would be approaching unseen. Walking

across the road would leave me exposed, and the last thing I wanted was for him to see his handiwork in my ruined clothes and ash-filled hair.

A transport approached from down the road and slowed, preparing to turn into the body shop. The solution hit me a second before I moved, sprinting toward the side of the vehicle. I knocked on the window. With a single word, the passenger ordered his transport to halt and warily lowered his window.

"They're, uh . . ." I glanced at the open garage bay. "They're cleaning up a mess inside. Big explosion earlier, lots of debris. I'll take your vehicle around back. You wait inside."

His mouth curled in disgust as he looked me over. Only then did I realize how clean and new this transport was.

"Were you in the middle of it?" he asked, his tone disapproving.

I forced a chuckle. "Yeah, it was pretty bad. I'm fine, though."

"Better clean it when you're done, then," the man muttered, unfastening his harness. I pulled the door open for him like I'd seen Travers do a dozen times. He slid out and strode toward the customer entrance without another word, shaking his head.

The second he looked away, I jumped inside. I couldn't believe it had actually worked. The old me, the Firebrand me, would have demanded he hand over the vehicle.

"Bay two," I ordered the transport—two bays away from the talking couple, just far enough they wouldn't suspect anything, but hopefully close enough to overhear. The transport pulled in and idled, awaiting my next command. The garage smelled of battery acid, old rubber, and melted cheese. It had to be lunchtime. That explained the empty bays and the Chadd guy's timing for this little meeting.

I moved to hit the power button, then thought better of it. If this went bad, I'd need a quick escape. Keeping my head ducked below the window, I leaned closer to hear.

". . . Firebrands never make guarantees like that," the woman was saying. "We're in the middle of a war, in case you hadn't noticed."

"Your idea of war is very different from ours."

I straightened and then remembered to duck again. I knew that voice. It had to be Chadd, or whatever his real name was.

The woman snorted. "Your kind can't think past their next meal, much less into tomorrow and beyond. You'll have to trust that we know what we're doing."

"With all due respect, if that were true, you wouldn't be here right now."

I strained to hear, but their conversation stopped. I willed them to continue. All I knew was that neither seemed happy about the prospect of working with the other. If the woman was a Firebrand, who was Chadd? What role did he play in this so-called war? Was she the person behind the fire last night?

The Firebrand's head appeared at the window. A sinister smile crept across her face.

Every curse word I'd ever learned escape my lips. "Transport, hospital! Emergency speed." It was the only destination that overrode a vehicle's programming and speed protocols.

"I heard what you did this morning, Kole," she called as the transport whipped backward. "We'll find you and take our revenge. As for your rich little girlfriend, you'd better pray Dane kills her quickly."

My vehicle plunged toward the street. All the while, the Firebrand's laughter followed me. I expected the clang of stun shots as well, but there was nothing—because she didn't have one or because she wanted me to escape? No sign of Chadd either. I swore again.

You'd better pray Dane kills her quickly.

They wanted Legacy—not to kidnap her and take full control of the country but to kill her outright. I had to warn her right away.

Then I would never leave her side again.

TEN

KOLE

Over an hour later, I reached Legacy's safe house and crept around to the back. I'd ditched the transport a few miles away and taken the long route, making a few extra rounds of the neighborhood to ensure no one followed. Once the hidden and disguised guards cleared me, I approached the door. Exhaustion took its toll now. I could barely lift my arm to knock.

The assistant who answered took in my appearance with wide eyes, then led me straight to Legacy's grandmother, who sat in her favorite chair. When I approached, she sat up so quickly I thought she'd fall right out of it. "Well, now. You've looked better."

I hid a little surprise of my own. I'd never seen the woman without her blankets, but here she sat, her trousers hanging loose over skeletal legs, her blouse not quite hiding her bony, narrow shoulders.

Gram lifted her blanket from the floor and threw it over her lap with a scowl. "It isn't polite to stare."

"It isn't polite to lie about your health either." I sat down on the sofa across from her, staying at the edge so I didn't get soot on the fabric, and eyed her blanket. "Cold, huh?"

A hint of color reached her pale cheeks. "Sometimes it's the cold. Other times . . ."

I understood what she wouldn't say. She didn't want Legacy to see the truth. "Are you sick?"

"Not sick, just old. Not a state I enjoy, if I'm being honest. All the excitement has made my brain think I'm still sixteen and having adventures."

"You wouldn't call this an adventure, would you?"

"An adventure is what you call it when it's all over. Right now, the people I love most are in danger and the future is uncertain. Appearances are all I can offer right now." She stroked her blanket, speaking softly. "The time for truth will come later."

I nodded. In her own way, Treena Hawking still held the country together. Legacy needed her, so Gram made sure she was there. If her health declined further, though . . . I felt sick at the thought. Losing Gram would destroy Legacy.

Gram sniffed and grimaced. "Speaking of appearances, there's a shower upstairs. I'll send some clean clothes up. Then we'll have a chat."

I looked around. "First, I have to tell Legacy something. Is she here?"

"Finally sleeping. I will not have her woken up, even for you. Shame you didn't think to check in with her after the fire. She's been through enough uncertainty without thinking her boyfriend is dead."

I groaned. Yet another stupid decision of the many I'd made today. "I have to tell her. She needs to know how sorry I am."

"When she wakes up. That girl thinks she can survive

on two hours of sleep a night, but it's bound to catch up with her. Meanwhile, we'll have our chat—after you get cleaned up."

———

FIFTEEN MINUTES LATER, I trotted downstairs feeling like a new person. My ribs still ached, but I'd taken some painkillers from the cabinet and seen to the scrapes on my legs and feet. There was little I could do about the bruising.

I hoped Legacy would be waiting for me when I reached the living room again, but it was Gram who met me, still in her chair. This time, a pile of blankets covered her lap. On the coffee table sat a plate of steaming potatoes and a mound of pulled meat. I feigned nonchalance, but my stomach betrayed me by releasing a growl that resembled a dying bear's.

An amused light entered Treena's eyes. "Sit and eat."

I knew better than to tell our country's founder no. I pulled at my shirt sleeves, which didn't quite reach my wrists, and took my earlier place on the sofa. A few bites in and I didn't care what Gram wanted to talk about. I wolfed the food down and examined the plate, tempted to lick it clean.

Gram snapped her fingers and told the assistant who entered to bring more. "You ready to talk?"

Ready to listen, more like, if I knew the woman at all. I thanked the assistant and sat back in my seat. "Shoot."

"You're the independent type. I respect that. Hawking women tend to fall for the strong ones, and I wouldn't want anything less for my Legacy. But you need to think about whether you're the best thing for her right now."

I nearly choked. "What?"

"My spies tell me Legacy was at your apartment a few hours before the fire started. Since she stomped out in a huff, I'm assuming you had another fight. I think we both agree that's fortunate considering the circumstances."

Did she honestly think that didn't haunt me every second? "I'm well aware of what could have happened, thank you."

"Do you know who started that fire and why?"

"I have a suspicion," I said, feeling too defensive to explain my theory just now. Until I knew for certain, I'd let her spies—the spies that had apparently hidden outside my building without my knowing—concoct their own wild stories. How many times had I crossed the neighborhood, making sure I wasn't followed, thinking we were safe? No wonder that Chadd guy found me so easily.

Gram's sharp eyes watched me. "We're both worried for Legacy's safety. I understood your insistence on your living in solitude. You believed the distance would keep her safe. Now that the danger has drawn nearer, your solution is to run to her and offer protection. I'd like your assurance that it won't put her in more danger."

That stopped me. I clasped my hands together and clenched my jaw, thinking for a long moment. Legacy meant everything to me. She was the one solid, real, dependable thing in my life while everything else fell away. But I had no idea how to explain that to a woman who'd practically stopped a world war and assembled a nation from nothing. I felt insignificant under her gaze. A guy from the Shadows, no job and no income, in love with a granddaughter who, for some reason, kept me around. I felt the older woman's eyes on me, waiting.

"All I can promise is that I'll protect her with my life," I finally said.

"And if they take your life and she's still exposed, what then?"

I clenched my jaw and looked her in the eye. "Then I'll make sure she has other guards around to back me up."

"At all times?"

"Always."

She nodded. "Good. Now, for the other problem. When she came home last night, she wouldn't say a word and didn't sleep a wink. I'd like to know what you said to upset her."

"What I said?" Suddenly I felt like a defendant on trial. Did she have a mental list of my wrongdoings and insufficiencies? "Look, Legacy and I disagree on a lot of things. Sometimes it's hard for her to not get what she wants. She . . ." I nearly told her about Chadd right then just to show Gram how I'd kept Legacy from harm, but there were a hundred ways that interaction could have gone wrong. I didn't want to sink myself any deeper. "She has strong opinions."

"I see." Gram's eyes crinkled at the corners, an expression I now recognized as an attempt to hide a smile. "Hawkings have strong opinions about the things that matter—the Rating system, for instance. As a Firebrand, you once pushed for it. What are your feelings now?"

Oh, boy. The way things were going, I'd be tossed out by dusk. Something told me she would see through a lie, though, so I answered honestly. "My feelings have changed plenty, but I do think the Rating system had some advantages over the current system."

She seemed surprised at my honesty. "Such as?"

"You claim to offer freedom, but we're stuck in a single profession forever, even if interests change. Everyone wants to climb the professional ladder, but when no upper positions open up, most people get caught at the bottom with minimal income their entire lives. At least with the Rating system, people could work harder to get their scores up and improve their situation."

She nodded thoughtfully. "Go on."

"Since most of us are relegated to the worst jobs, we get poor housing in the Shadows. That means rolling blackouts and cheap surplus groceries and second-rate medical care. We rely on public transportation and walking to get anywhere, which means we're often late for work or school. And when positions at work do open up, we have to hide our growling stomachs and worn clothing and put on a fake smile to compete with the upper classes. It almost never works. Not to mention that in the original NORA, your Enforcers patrolled the poorer areas more often to control crime. Here, it's the opposite. We aren't worth their time. We're left to live and eat and sleep in fear." I thought of the countless nights I'd lain awake in my bed, knowing that if my father came home drunk and ready for a fight, nobody would come to our rescue. I leaned forward. "So it isn't just individuals who suffer in poverty—it's their children and children's children. With all due respect, you've caused a generational problem and then punished us for the consequences."

Legacy's grandmother watched me, her eyes sharp and calculating.

"You did ask," I said, sitting back and resting my feet on the coffee table. Then I realized how bad my feet looked and lowered them to the floor.

"You're right," she said softly.

"Pardon?"

She raised her voice. "I didn't fix all the problems. I

made things better but not perfect. Legacy has a tough job ahead of her."

"So you believe she'll win and take the Copper Office back?"

"I do."

I frowned. "What about your son?"

An expression of raw pain crossed her face. It reflected my own so perfectly I instantly felt bad for the question.

"I'll see you tomorrow," Gram said, dodging the question. "Eat that second plate of food making its way down the hall right now, then my assistant will show you to your room. You look like you could sleep for ten years." She pushed to her feet with a grunt, letting her blankets fall to the floor, then kicked them aside and headed for the stairs.

"Would you like me to bring those up for you?" I asked.

She turned and gave me a wide, brilliant smile. "Be careful, Firebrand. I may grow to like you." She winked, then started up the steps.

ELEVEN

LEGACY

When I stumbled out of my room, I nearly tripped over a body in the hallway. Kole grunted, then pushed himself to his feet, his eyes as wide as his grin.

I stared at him, disbelieving, wondering if I were still dreaming. But I couldn't have dreamt up the burns on his forehead, the mischievous light in his eyes, or the unfamiliar white shirt with its faded stains. Kole was here. He was okay.

A delighted squeal escaped my throat, chasing away some of the darkness inside. I threw myself at him, nearly knocking him over again.

"Whoa there," he said, wrapping his so-very-real arms around me. "Look, I'm sorry I didn't contact you afterward. I'm such an idiot. Of course, you wouldn't know I escaped. There was something I had to take care of, and . . . did I mention I'm an idiot?"

I wanted to agree with him, but I couldn't make light of the hours I'd spent worrying I would never see him again. Just like Mom. There one day, gone the next. He wouldn't understand, and I didn't want to make him either. Not when he stood here, alive and repentant and wonderful, bruises and burns and all.

"Why didn't you come in and wake me?" I asked.

He chuckled, stroking my back with one hand. "Your grandmother threatened me with execution by torture if I even touched your door."

That sounded like her. I stamped down the adrenaline rushing through my veins and let myself melt into him once more. I drew in a long breath, taking in the essence of him. He smelled of soap and the faintest hint of smoke. That brought reality crashing onto my shoulders. "Sounds like you had a tough night."

He stiffened but didn't pull away. "I've had better." A lifetime of pain hung heavy in his voice. It reminded me of the first day I'd spoken with him, on the last day of school. He had always seemed different from the other guys, more somber, maybe a little angry. Now that I knew a little more about his background and understood the anger that drove him, I felt more helpless than ever. Kole was an orphan in more ways than one. I'd taken him from everything he ever knew—his uncle, his friends, his former life.

I hoped the trade was a good one. So far, I wasn't convinced.

Kole pulled back slightly and brushed my cheek with his finger. "What's wrong?"

I nearly laughed at the irony of his question but gave a heavy sigh instead. Had he missed so much since yesterday? "General Knox isn't coming. I can't ask my supporters to fight when they've already suffered so much. We've already begun to ration meals, and people are sleeping on the floor, not to mention the patients they've brought to us are no better than they were before. We haven't made any strides with the implant problem. I've hit one dead end after another."

He took my elbows and brushed his thumbs across them, sending a delighted shiver through my body. "Your supporters joined you to fight, Legacy. They deserve that chance." He paused. "There's something else. I think Dane is contacting the Shadow gangs for support. I saw a Firebrand speaking with one of them this morning, and he looked an awful lot like your Chadd friend. I think he's the one who started the fire last night."

Dread made me stiffen, but something in Kole's voice stopped me. "It looked like him or was him?"

A flicker of uncertainty crossed his face. "I only saw him from behind, but I'd swear it was him."

A few days ago, I would have accepted Kole's word without question. But today something made me pause, and I didn't like it. Did Kole truly see that stranger from the doorstep, or did he simply want to be right? How much could I trust a mind I loved but knew was broken and growing worse all the time?

I hated this. I hated Virgil for hurting the guy who meant everything to me, especially considering what Kole had given up for me. Most of all, I hated that, for the first time in our relationship, I couldn't trust him with everything.

"We'll watch for him, then," I told Kole gently, hoping he'd drop the subject.

He shook his head. "Not good enough. I talked to the Firebrand he met with. Legacy, I think Dane has orders to kill you."

That brought us to the last topic I wanted to discuss. I steeled myself, all too aware of his watching for my reaction. "I think you're right about that." Then I told him about our harrowing transport chase and escape, leaving out the most terrifying details.

His face grew darker with every word. When I finished, he pushed past me and stalked toward the stairs. "That's it. I'm having a little chat with Travers."

I grabbed his arm. "He feels bad enough already. Besides, it was my choice."

"Until you decide to listen to me about the danger we're facing, I'm taking that choice away. From now on, you don't go anywhere without me. I've already discussed it with Gram."

Frustration welled up inside me like bile. "Gram doesn't get to decide that, and neither do you. I'm trying to run a movement here."

"Yes," he hissed. "And we're trying to help you do it. Don't make our job harder. We don't have enough people to win this, let alone chase you around the city when you think you're invincible. If Alex gets ahold of you again, you're never coming back." There was a crazed edge to his voice.

"Your job?" I snapped. "I didn't know spending time with me was such a burden for you."

"I stayed away to protect you, not because I don't want to be with you. I thought if I kept Dane's attention off you, you'd be safer." He looked hurt. "Clearly, I was wrong about that."

An angry retort leaped to mind, but the devastation on his face stopped me. This paranoia—was it the protectiveness of a boyfriend or the fear of the orphan who'd lost everyone else he loved? Did Kole mean to help me win this war or keep me out of it completely? Grandpa Vance had been a steadying influence on Gram, but I couldn't recall him ever standing in her way. I wasn't sure what that meant for us.

I switched tactics. "You really mean to follow me every-where? The washroom, the meeting room?" I lowered my voice. "My room?"

That mischievous light entered his eyes again. He brushed my forehead with a kiss. "Everywhere you'll let me," he said in a husky voice, only half teasing.

I stroked his rough jawline, imagining what he had been through since I saw him last. There was something new in his eyes, a kind of sorrow and wisdom that hadn't been there yesterday. "I'm glad you're okay," I told him softly. "Have you seen the physician yet, just to make sure?"

"I'm fine." He avoided my gaze, which meant he was far from fine. "It's just that I'm glad you weren't there."

I felt his hand slide around my waist, and he pulled me against him once more. Then his lips were on mine, hungry and insistent. I responded by pulling him closer, my hand on his chest where his Firebrand tattoo hid, my fingers snaking up to his neck and through his hair, and then there was only him, everywhere and always.

Voices sounded downstairs, demanding my attention. I reluctantly pulled my head away, gasping for breath, but Kole moved to my cheek, my throat. If I didn't stop him, we'd go on forever. There was work to be done.

Someday the fate of thousands of people wouldn't stand between us. I longed for that so desperately I could hardly breathe.

"Well, at least we still have this," Kole said, his voice raspy. "After last night, I wasn't sure."

"Neither was I." I didn't want to talk about last night ever again.

He watched me sadly. "This movement isn't the only thing that's broken, is it?"

I didn't know how to answer that. Our fighting seemed

to dominate our conversations these days, and I saw no end to it in the future if Kole truly meant to follow me around like a trained dog.

"Broken things can still be beautiful," I told him.

He looked at me in wonder. "You're absolutely right."

But before he could continue, a pounding on the stairs drove us farther apart. Foster appeared, breathless. He gave a quick bow that looked more like a bob. "Your Honor, I have news."

"Kole is alive," I said for him, sliding out of Kole's arms. "He's fine."

Foster barely spared him a glance. "No, Your Honor. Something else. Something bad."

The panic in his eyes sent my heart galloping again. "Yes?"

"It's the warehouse, Your Honor. It's been attacked."

TWELVE
LEGACY

I TORE my harness off and threw open the transport door to leap out before we even stopped, earning a frown from Travers. He'd insisted on using a worn transport at least fifteen years old and surrounding us with other vehicles full of guards. The ride here had been agonizingly slow. I stumbled to a halt in front of the smoking hunk of wreckage that had once been our lab and temporary hospital. It looked as if someone had set off a bomb. The building's remains were charred and smoking, and a relentless heat radiated from the heap of rubble. Even the building next to it sported black walls and a partially melted roof.

A crowd stood behind a makeshift barrier near the narrow road that led to the main street. It seemed like half the neighborhood. My guards jumped out of the car and either took positions along the barrier or headed for the wreckage to look for survivors.

I could barely stand here, a dozen meters away, without the heat singing my flesh. There wouldn't be any survivors.

My brother's message was loud and clear.

I will destroy everything you build. Stand down, or more people will get hurt.

A figure broke away from the wreckage and hurried toward me. To my disappointment, it wasn't Millian but the older woman who'd approached her yesterday while we spoke. Her hair was pasted to her head, her cheeks lined with ash.

"The patients," I said breathlessly. "Are they all accounted for?"

"Every one, Your Honor." She bobbed her head. "The Firebrands helped them evacuate while they destroyed the lab. The moment our last patient set foot outside, they lit everything aflame. We moved them to an empty house around the corner till we got instructions from you, but we're missing most of the stabilization equipment, though we don't have reliable power there anyhow. We'll need a better option."

"What about the homeless group that arrived earlier?"

"All fine. They're there as well."

I felt all the air escape my lungs. At least that little boy would be all right. As for the comatose patients, Alex had to know that killing the country's most vulnerable citizens wouldn't reflect well on him. But our research had been an attempt to help them too, and now it was all gone—along with any chance of helping Dad. The memory of Millian's neatly organized room with its cataloged experiments and clean tables made me swallow hard. Kole reached my side and took my hand, squeezing it.

"And Millian?" I asked the woman in a shaky voice. "Where is she?"

"Physician Redd said her injuries needed special attention, so he ordered her transported to the unit caring for His

Honor Hawking." She bowed again, this time so deeply she practically kissed her heat-singed shoes.

That meant Millian would be on her way to the safe house. Kole and I shared a look of dread. "Injuries?" I repeated.

"Yes, Your Honor. Director Comondor tried to stand up to the arsonists. Shot a few of them before they stunned her. The rest of us ran. I—I don't know how to fight." She seemed ashamed. "The ones she hit haven't woken up yet." She pointed toward another building across the street.

Prisoners. We needed to interrogate them, see what we could learn about Alex's orders.

I started to move, but Kole grabbed my hand tighter. "I'll handle them. You wait here with your guards. I'll meet you at the transport in twenty minutes."

I blinked at him, puzzled, but he strode away without another word. The only reason he'd agree to leave my side was because he worried about my safety. Clearly, he thought the Firebrand prisoners dangerous, bound or not. I considered going after him and insisting he stop issuing orders and let me do what needed to be done. But as I stared at the wreckage before me, the fight drained away.

Fire. It was always fire. First Mom's destroyed lab, then my failed attempt to stop Virgil. Now the Firebrands' vicious echo of the past, like a constant reminder of my personal shortcomings.

"Did they take anything?" I asked the lab assistant, who had turned to watch the billowing white smoke rise into the sky. She had flakes of gray ash in her hair, much like the glass I'd brushed free in my hair earlier. Had that really been just this morning?

"They stole a few boxes from the lab," she said, "but I don't know what was inside. They didn't save a single piece of medical equipment. We lost it all. That's what made Director Comondor really angry. She chased them down and nearly got those boxes back before they set that cannon up."

I stiffened. "What cannon?"

She looked alarmed at my sudden interest. "Pardon, Your Honor. I shouldn't call it a cannon, exactly. More like a huge stunner, but I've never seen the likes of it. Four medical assistants ran inside after the evacuation to try and save the medical equipment, but they didn't reach the doors before those Firebrands blasted them."

Another stun cannon. Not good. "Where are the medical assistants now?"

She shifted and pointed a few meters away where a clump of what I'd assumed was wreckage finally became clear. All I could make out was a charred boot.

First my attack, and now the murders of innocent medical professionals. Alex's obsession with winning had reached a new low. If they'd made a stun cannon by increasing the size of a stunner, what else could they be working on? How far would my brother go to hold on to his power?

Who else would we lose before the end?

My eyes watered, and not just from the smoke. I turned to Foster, who had arrived with the two council members. They slowly climbed out of the transport and somberly inspected the wreckage.

"We need a safer place for the patients and the homeless," I told Foster. "See what you can find."

He nodded and lowered his voice. "The island? The specialists have cleared the tunnel for passage and the hotel for lodging. I believe they were testing the water there when this happened." He gestured to the lab's remains.

Just thinking about the massive effort of transporting everyone there made my head ache. "Not yet. Let's buy the specialists a little more time to complete their investigation. We'll need a temporary solution in the meantime. We also need more medical equipment. Find a medical assistant to help identify what we need and where we can get it."

"I'll see what I can do." He eyed the four bodies on the ground. "And them?"

"Notify their families. We'll let them come for them." I didn't like it, but bringing the bodies to their loved ones would be too dangerous with Firebrands roaming the city. We'd stayed too long already. "Please give them my thanks. These assistants likely saved lives in their work."

Foster nodded, looking a little sick.

I turned to Travers. "Please tell Kole when he returns that I'm going to visit the patients and make sure they're situated. Then we'll go home. I need to check on Millian right away."

———

PHYSICAN REDD WAS LEAVING as we arrived home. He assured me Millian would be fine. She'd probably suffered a concussion, but the scans showed no broken bones. She would soon be awake.

Kole helped me move her to an empty bedroom, then excused himself and disappeared into his own room. It was then I realized he hadn't said much on the way home. Exhaustion, perhaps? Or maybe frustration at how little information he'd gleaned from the Firebrand prisoners?

Guilt flooded my chest as the answer struck me. Those Firebrands had likely once been his friends. I hadn't even considered how it would feel to suddenly be on the other side, demanding answers, inflicting pain. I thought about Alex and imagined torturing him for information. It was unthinkable. No matter how stupid my Alex acted, he would always be my brother.

Once Millian was situated, I made my way down the quiet hall to Dad's room and sat on the stool next to his bed. He looked exactly as he had this morning, pale and still, his mouth in a gentle frown. Tubes ran into his nose from an oxygen tank at my side. Two other machines beeped gently, monitoring his functions. Until a couple of hours ago, dozens of the patients in our hospital looked exactly like this. Now, without the equipment we needed, most lay unplugged and were completely on their own. I hadn't had time to ask Physician Redd what that meant for them.

I took Dad's hand in mine. It felt limp and cold. I placed my other hand on top of it and tried to warm it, but it was a lost cause. My dad, larger than life, the man who had all the answers, lay still in bed with his eyes closed. Today, Sleeping Beauty wasn't a princess but the king. It wasn't a prince he waited upon but his princess daughter—and it wasn't a kiss that would awaken him but a cure.

A cure that may as well be buried in miles of Antarctic ice because I would never find it now.

For the first time, the very real possibility of losing him hit me square in the face. Mom's death had carved a hollow section from my chest where my heart once resided. Alex's betrayal had dug a knife into my chest. What would losing Dad feel like? Could I bear any more pain without breaking completely?

My hand gripped his so tightly it would have hurt him had he been awake. As if taunting me, his fingers remained white and cold. Meanwhile, my own had turned a bright, angry red and purple.

"I'm a terrible leader," I told Dad. "If I'd placed more guards like I said I would, maybe the warehouse would still be standing."

My words were met only by silence, just like always. The same silence that filled our home during the past year with Mom gone. The silence of a dinner table filled with food only Alex and I would eat because Dad had locked himself in his room, companion only to his own grief. The silence he demanded from me whenever the topic of my future came up and the silence of keeping secrets about my past. And now the silence of distance, because although he lay right here next to me, he felt as unreachable as Mom.

A wave of new anger flung me to my feet, shocking me with its intensity. I dropped his hand and stood over him. "You don't get to lie there and sleep through all of this. It isn't fair. You're supposed to be leading them. You, not me. Thanks for thinking I could do this, but I can't, and I know that now, and I . . . I want you here." My voice wavered, and I swallowed the pain back. "We need you. *I* need you. Please wake up."

There was no acknowledgment of my desperation, no assurance that everything would be okay. Nothing that a parent would give to a suffering child.

"Please," I whispered, but it wasn't my dad I spoke to now. It was the empty, quiet walls. It was Grandpa Vance and Mom and everyone else who'd gone into the darkness and never returned.

I was so, so tired of the darkness that never answered back.

The thought made my anger return. I picked up one of Dad's shoes off the floor and threw it at the wall. It hit it with a thud, leaving a tiny black mark. I didn't feel a single ounce better than before.

I listened for a minute to see if anyone would come and lecture me like I was a noisy child, but, to my disappointment, nobody did. Even if they had, they would've bowed and left the room in silence because of who I was supposed to be. A thousand supporters depended on me, and half the city opposed Alex right along with me, yet I'd never felt more alone.

Did Alex feel alone too? Did he feel the loss of our family as keenly as I did? Did he even realize the damage he'd done to both of us today?

I took Dad's cold hand again, a hardened resolve filling me now. I loved my brother, and I didn't want to hurt him, but he had gone too far today.

I would never again allow him to hurt the people I loved.

Never.

THIRTEEN

KOLE

THE PAIN FELT like an electric current searing through my body one cell at a time. I was cold and hot, sharp blades and disintegrating and melting all at once. Deep in the back of my mind, I knew the pain only existed in my head, but that didn't matter. The sensations tearing me apart piece by excruciating piece were very real.

But the emotions were far worse.

"Don't," my mother said, cowering against the wall. "We'll talk about this tomorrow when you're feeling better. Please."

"I'm feeling fine, and we'll talk about it now." The deep voice coming from my lips, distant and ice-cold, was my father's. The belt's leather felt rough beneath my fingers. My throat burned worse than the rest of me, whether from his drinking or my desperation to escape, I couldn't tell.

My arm raised the belt as if on its own. Then it came down sharp, hard. A cry tore from my mother's mouth, but she didn't scream. Not yet. That part would come later.

The familiarity of it all tickled something in my mind. How many times had I seen this, *lived* this, before?

Wake up. It's a dream.
Wake.
Up.

A yelp and a streak of blood on my mother's face. She turned her shoulder to me, folding herself to protect her face—a face that gazed on me with tenderness from my very first days. But now . . . I struggled against the other thoughts, the bad ones, as they overcame my mind.

Disgusting creature. She was beautiful once, strong even. But now she whimpers like a child when she doesn't get her way and lies and hides my credits around the house. I've been patient enough. Time to show her that kind of behavior will never be tolerated here.

With a roar, I swung the belt again. It hit her on the shoulder this time, making her flinch, but her head and face were still protected. She turned to look at me as I pulled the belt back for another strike, the fear in her eyes fading as something else—a flash of anger—replaced it.

She may as well have lit a match. Rage burned through my veins again, sending a sharp pain through my head in the form of a migraine. The belt obviously wasn't enough. It would take far too long to make my point.

Somewhere deep inside, I cringed, knowing exactly what came next. I was powerless to stop it.

Wake up!

It wouldn't work, I lamented from somewhere deep inside my head. It never did.

My fingers closed around the drawer pull on my nightstand. They knew exactly where to find the knife.

Mom, run!

The words didn't leave my lips, but to my surprise, she met my gaze for a moment. There was understanding along with the anger, as if she knew what lay beneath my—

rather, my father's—demeanor. Then she sprang for the doorway.

Growling, I moved to block her, but she was too fast. I lunged for her arm, which slid through my fingers until I caught her hand. A small, sharp object dug into my palm. Her wedding ring. I pulled her off balance, and she stumbled, throwing herself back toward the door, her eyes wide and desperate and still very much alive and *not learning her lesson.*

And then her face changed. It was no longer my mother who stood panting before me but Legacy, her long dark hair tumbling down her shoulders. So beautiful. So terrified. Looking utterly, horribly betrayed.

My arm lifted, the blade pointing downward, and her mouth opened in an endless scream.

"You're scaring me. Kole. Wake up."

My eyes flung open to find Legacy kneeling above me, a hard wood floor beneath me, my father's knife nowhere in sight.

The only thing that remained of my nightmare was the fear in Legacy's eyes.

I looked around the room again, but it did little to calm my nerves. Furniture lay toppled all around me, and a cool breeze wafted in through the window. Strange. I didn't remember leaving it open.

Then I saw the glass covering the floor. A thousand shards, a million, all glinting in the blue light coming in from the brilliant sky above. The pain hit a second later, and I let my gaze drop to my hand. My right fist was a bloody mess.

"What in the fates?" I murmured.

"Exactly my reaction." She sounded stern, but her voice wobbled a bit.

If this unnerved her, it was a good thing she couldn't see inside my head. "Just a nightmare. It happens all the time."

She looked around the room again. "Does it?" she asked softly.

I rose to my feet without answering, giving the room another quick sweep. It wasn't just the furniture I'd damaged. One wall had a distinct dent that hadn't been there last night. My blanket looked even worse, tattered as if a mutt had been locked in here for weeks and tried to eat his way out. Or perhaps someone had taken a shredder to it. I looked around again and found my knife on the floor. I gave it a little kick, sending it under the bed.

"Did this happen before your incident at Neuromen?" she asked, a cautious tone in her voice.

I ignored the question, thinking about yesterday's arsonist interrogation. It had taken longer than it should have to discover that those Firebrands knew very little about Dane's plan, and it hadn't been exactly pleasant. Surely that had triggered this and nothing more.

"I'll clean this up," I told her. "Gram will never know it happened. I'll see you at breakfast, okay? Try to get some sleep."

She gaped at me now. "You nearly tore the house down, and you're telling me to go back to bed? Kole, this is not normal. Is this why you wanted your own apartment, for when you do . . . whatever this is?"

The last thing I needed was a therapy session right now. "It's like I told you. It was just a nightmare."

"And how many times over the past weeks have you turned into destructo-monster in your sleep? Don't you dare lie to me."

I gritted my teeth. "You have nothing to worry about, all

right? I'm fine. You're fine. Nobody else woke up. It's not a big deal."

She stared at me incredulously.

I swiped a piece of the blanket off the floor and pressed it to my hand to stop the bleeding. That would be hard to hide in the morning. Same with the broken glass and the dent in the wall. Maybe if I kept people out of here until we switched bases again, nobody else would notice.

"Unbelievable." Legacy started for the door.

"Wait."

She turned around and folded her arms. "Why, are you going to tell me the truth?"

I hesitated.

Legacy raised an eyebrow in the moonlight.

"I don't know when it started," I admitted. It was all I could give her right now. "But I would never hurt you. You know that, right?"

"Of course I know that."

"Good. Then let's forget about all this and focus on more important things."

She stared at me for a long moment, shook her head, and left.

That went well. The anger from my nightmare hadn't dissipated completely nor the ache in my skull it always brought, and I took a few long breaths to clear my head. The cold air from the broken window helped. I took another look around, decided there wasn't much I could do tonight, and entered the hallway, careful to close the door.

I would never hurt Legacy, at least not intentionally. But that didn't mean I would never lie to her.

There was more than one way to protect someone you loved.

As a child, I'd walked the city at night and looked for

the stars far beyond the thick, gray clouds. Occasionally, one would peek through as if taunting me with its distance. It was those stars, the strong ones, I wished upon. I never voiced the wish because Mom said doing so would render the star powerless, and it needed all the power it could get to grant my wish. Never mind that my wishes never came true anyway.

Today, it wasn't a wish I didn't dare voice but reality. Some truths couldn't be spoken. That would grant them power over my life, and I would never, ever relinquish that power.

"I should have slept on the street," I muttered, heading down the stairs. It wouldn't be the first time. There were worse things than curling up in the shadows of a quiet street and hearing cats fighting and crickets singing their pulsating tune and feeling one with the city as the cold night air penetrated my skin. Yes, I'd seen much worse things.

I couldn't imagine anything worse than what I'd seen in Legacy's eyes tonight.

FOURTEEN
LEGACY

I LAY in bed long after Kole's footsteps faded down the hallway. Any other night, I would have joined him. But tonight I'd watched the guy I loved crack apart and then lie to my face. He was as far from okay as a person could be yet refused to admit it. His health would forever be the shadow in the corner we both denied existed. Except I couldn't pretend much longer.

Physician Redd was right. Kole had begun to unravel in an alarming way, and I couldn't talk to anyone about it.

I gave a long sigh and threw my arm over my eyes, blocking out the moonlight coming through the window. It didn't help.

The movement isn't the only thing that's broken, Kole had said.

He would never agree to go under like Dad. After what happened to his mom, he'd never voluntarily lie in a hospital bed again. He wouldn't even lie down on a sofa without watching the door, probably envisioning a dozen scenarios in which intruders entered and he fought them off. Anxiety,

I'd thought, or maybe PTSD. But now that he'd escaped a burning building, his senses were in a continual high state of alert.

I could never convince him of his safety. Maybe not even when this was all over. What would be left for us, then? Was this the Kole—the guy who smashed glass in his sleep and threw furniture—I wanted by my side in war and in peace?

I thought of that image capture of Mom and Dad during their engagement hidden somewhere in my room a dimension away. Dad's mischievous smile as he carried her on his back. The laughter in Mom's eyes and her mouth open in an exclamation of delight, her arms wrapped securely around his shoulders. So free. So easy. That was what love meant.

Nothing about Kole and me was easy these days. I didn't know what to think of that.

There was no sound from downstairs. Either Kole was still there or he'd gone for a walk in the dead of night. Probably the latter.

I put my shoes on and crept down the steps, placing my feet carefully to avoid the squeaking floorboards. The main room stood empty, and the air felt slightly cooler here on my bare arms. He'd snuck outside, then. I ached to go to him, to tell him we'd get through this together. That I'd be there for him the way he'd been there for me. It was all true . . . but it also wasn't. Because I couldn't help him if he refused to help himself.

I felt torn between two forces—a country that desperately needed help I couldn't give, and a guy who needed me but pretended he didn't.

Plopping down at the kitchen table, I put my head in my hands. Paper crinkled beneath my elbow. I frowned and pulled it out. That hadn't been there last night. A note from Kole?

I flipped the light on and squinted at the messy, barely coherent scrawl. Definitely not the neat, intentional handwriting Kole used.

I NEED TO GO HOME SOON BUT I WANT TO TELL YOU WHAT

    YOU NEED TO NOWE YOU WILL BELEVE ME WHEN YOU SEE.

    YOU ARENT ALONE YOU HAVE ALLIES TO HELP.

    MIDNIGHT WENSDAY WERE IT ALL BEGAN.

    PLEASE.

I read it several times before letting myself breathe again. I took another look around, but nothing else in the room stood amiss. If the author of this message was still here, he'd hidden himself well. And I was fairly certain I knew who it was.

Chadd. The last person to arrive before his building burned down. The one Kole claimed he'd seen yesterday talking to a Firebrand. He'd found us.

A warning, perhaps? If I didn't meet the guy, would he burn down this home as well?

With a frown, I read the note again. Even if Kole was wrong about yesterday, this guy had found me twice. That made him dangerous, no matter how innocent his note seemed. This could be an attempt to get me alone so they could bring me straight to Alex.

But why leave this note, then? He could have kidnapped me from my bed or turned all of us in at once. It wouldn't take long to storm the building and arrest everyone. Firebrands didn't knock on doors and make up elaborate stories or sneak into homes to leave letters. They just took what they wanted and ran. And Firebrands *never* said please. Besides, Kole could be wrong about what he saw. After all, he'd just destroyed a room in his sleep and denied a problem existed.

I looked toward the door, knowing exactly what Kole would say if I showed him. He would get all the more protective and refuse to let me even consider meeting the guy. And after tonight . . . My heart squeezed a little. Kole wasn't okay. I couldn't allow him to make decisions for the entire movement when he couldn't even make the right decisions for himself.

I thought of the warehouse and the wealth of information we'd lost last night. One more mistake and we'd lose more than a building, equipment, and four medical assistants. It wasn't even a matter of whether but when. As long as we remained in the city, we would get caught. Even if Millian's plan worked and we converted the entire city to my side, we could lose this war. It was time to move from defense to offense, from NORA to the island. Time to gather our forces and prepare for war.

You aren't alone, the note said. *You have allies to help.*

This guy couldn't have known how desperately I needed those words.

I read it again, memorizing it. "Where it began" could only mean one place. I crumpled the note in my palm, walked to the stove, and tossed it in. The flame, orange, red, and brilliant purple, sprang to life within its secure box.

The note glowed brightly as the flame surrounded it, its edges turning brown. Then the two were one—the paper being consumed, the fire devouring. I'd spent the past few weeks like that paper, floating about and allowing myself to be used, burned, consumed. No longer.

This time, I would be the flame.

FIFTEEN

KOLE

I RETURNED to find chaos awaiting me.

A large transport blocked the back alley, *NORA's Best Affordable Heating & Air* scrawled across its side. Its back lay open to expose a ramp and several workers carrying boxes. Many of the guards I'd come to recognize had joined them, though they paused to watch me stalk up the lawn toward the door. It took talking to three people before I understood.

While I'd wandered the city last night, Legacy had decided to move everyone across the channel and awakened the entire house with a flurry of orders. She'd even brought people over from the shelters to help, some of whom looked a little more malnourished than the rest. Probably members of the homeless community I'd heard about. Even with all these people here, it was a wonder how much they'd accomplished.

Rather than clean up my mess and return to bed like I'd planned, I fell in step with the others, packing and carrying boxes and supplies. When my stomach growled, I stole a few pieces of old bread from a kitchen box and plowed on.

Legacy's strange behavior had to have something to do with last night. I was certain of it.

It was late morning before Legacy appeared. She situated herself next to Gram to oversee the preparations, pretending not to watch me. Every time I met her gaze, she tore her eyes away.

The seconds till our next inevitable argument ticked by, disappearing into nothing, my dread building. I knew how that conversation would go—the word "coma" was sure to come up. Legacy always relied too heavily on her family physician's point of view. Probably her scientist mom's upbringing.

My upbringing was a little more practical. Fight to survive. Never leave yourself vulnerable. Stay away from food prepared by someone else. Always carry a weapon. I resisted the urge to pat the knife weighing down my right pocket.

As late morning unfolded into afternoon, Travers joined me. He intercepted the box in my hands and set it down, albeit too roughly. Then he leaned over. "If these chilly looks between the two of you continue, we won't need iceboxes for our food."

I grunted. Travers smirked and adjusted the box, then joined me at the pile to move another.

"Girls don't forget easily, do they?" I muttered.

Travers snorted, then covered it with a cough. He lifted a box and angled it between his face and Legacy across the room. "No, and there's no 'easily' about it. Learn that now, so you can enjoy your time together."

"I'm sorry about your wife," I said, imagining how it would feel to lose Legacy like that.

The older man grunted under the box's weight. "Thank you. Our relationship had more imperfection in it than perfection, I'm afraid, but I wouldn't have been happy with perfection anyway. She would be happy with our work here."

Sometimes it was hard to believe we *were* helping people. I understood Legacy's frustration with our lack of progress. "I'm here to keep Legacy safe, yet she hates me for it."

"It's the priceless birds who resent their cages most." He lifted the box into the truck, then sighed with relief as he turned to look at me. "Women like Legacy refuse to accept the worst from us. That's why they make the best partners."

Legacy certainly fit that description. I'd never met anyone like her. "It would be nice if she could trust me, though."

He snorted. "Make sure you've earned that trust before you demand it from her."

I scowled. "I've always trusted her. She knows that."

"Does she? Because that's the look of a woman who's trying to decide how to bash a guy over the head."

I looked at Legacy again, but she spoke with one of her assistants now. Her eyes flicked to me, then away again. The only indication of her anger was the pink in her cheeks.

"I may deserve that on occasion," I admitted. "She's just so different it's sometimes hard to understand her. We don't think the same about most things."

"She wouldn't like you if you did. Nobody wants to date a mirror image of themselves. They want someone who complements their strengths, and for her, that's you." He smirked again. "Apparently."

"But I don't get that. She grew up in a mansion with gourmet meals and transports and—well, drivers," I said pointedly. This entire conversation was weird, but having it with her driver made it even more strange. "I had one set of clothes, and they rarely fit right. When I walked to school in the rain, I'd arrive drenched, and the professors would yell at me, thinking I meant disrespect by it. Sometimes I went days without eating. I'd sneak through the dumpster at a restaurant and get yelled at by the manager. But they eventually went back inside, so I kept digging."

Travers thought for a long moment. "Those Hawkings love their comfortable lives, it's true. Most people would. But they also love people, deeply and passionately. I've known Legacy for years, and I'm telling you, she has a big heart. She just doesn't want anyone to know it."

"But what about after all this?" I gestured around us. "Say we win, which isn't likely. Where is my place in her life when she gets the Copper Office? They don't even have unvaccinated cats in their neighborhood, let alone a guy who's—who's done hard things to survive." I'd nearly let my secret slip. *A guy who killed his own father.*

"Couples make their own place. You'll find yours." Travers slapped me on the back. "In the meantime, your role is to help Legacy carry her load, not block her path. I imagine she has quite enough of that already with those council members and Gram's opinions."

I looked across the room at Legacy, who still spoke with her assistant. Her cheeks had turned a deep red now. Bad news? I took a step toward her, then paused. She wouldn't appreciate my barging into the issue right now. We had to mend what lay broken between us before she would allow me back into my role of supporter, and Travers was right about that. It was *all* I could be right now.

But how to mend a broken relationship? I'd never had to do that before.

I looked around the room once more. The piles of boxes

and furniture were rapidly diminishing. "Where is Legacy staying tonight?"

"Here. Said she had something to do in the morning and didn't want to travel all that way just to turn around and come back. Gram will accompany His Honorable Hawking and Millian to the island this afternoon, so it will be just you, me, and Miss Hawking here tonight. And her guards, of course."

I nodded thoughtfully. "There's some kind of cook preparing all your food, right?"

"An assistant who cooks, yes. But she's already crossed over to the island to prepare the kitchens. We'll be fending for ourselves until we join the others tomorrow."

"Perfect."

Legacy's driver cocked an eyebrow. "I don't follow."

I looked him in the eye. "You know I enjoy your company, but is there any chance I can persuade you to accompany Gram to the island instead? I'll radio you in the morning when we're ready to come over. I'm going to cook Legacy dinner, but don't say anything. I want to surprise her."

His confusion melted into understanding. "Of course. My lips are sealed, Firebrand. Just don't undercook it and give her food poisoning, or I'll find you."

I grinned. "Deal."

SIXTEEN

LEGACY

My escape went exactly as planned.

I slipped away shortly after the transport left, Gram and Travers trailing it in a different vehicle. Travers sent me a wave and a promise to return tomorrow. Kole had mysteriously disappeared. After all his talk of staying together, I waited a little while, concocting wild stories of why I needed to be alone tonight, none of which he would have believed.

The guard change finally forced my hand. It was now or never, so I slipped out and ducked behind the fence just as the new shift took their places, feeling a heavy guilt settle in my stomach. Kole would never forgive me for this, but I had to try. I'd never get another chance.

I arrived at the hospital several hours early, one hand on the stunner in my pocket as the sun dipped behind the line of structures forming the city skyline. The building loomed high overhead, at least ten stories tall with dark windows that reflected the city lights as they came on one by one. Well, most of the city, anyway. As the blue sky faded into purple, then gray, then black, the Shadows remained in darkness as always. Another policy I would ask Dad to change when he awoke.

What if he never wakes up? I shoved back the thought, but it floated there, ever in my mind.

After four times around the hospital, taking in the crisp coolness of the night and the calming song of crickets, I began to relax a little. No armies of Firebrands hid on the rooftop or deep in the bushes. If that messenger wanted to harm me, he hadn't set up my demise before now. Maybe he truly was who he claimed.

The possibilities set my heart galloping, but I pushed them back. Hope was dangerous.

I crossed the road and settled beneath the overhang of an office building. I could see anyone who arrived at the hospital from here, but they couldn't see me. With my back to the building, this position would also be decently easy to defend. I tightly gripped my stunner and glanced at the old-fashioned watch on my wrist. Midnight felt an eternity away.

I busied myself thinking of my favorite memories. It was a game Alex and I had played as children. We named an acquaintance of ours, the more distant the better, and told elaborate stories about this person with a single thread of truth. Then the other person had to guess which parts were lies. Alex usually won. I'd never been good at lying.

Midnight finally arrived. I visually swept the area. A cat crossed the street, then pounced on a tiny shadow. The shadow got away.

Twenty minutes passed. Then thirty.

Forty. Forty-five.

The stunner grew heavier with each passing minute. My fingers went slack as my head drooped, and I nearly dropped the weapon a couple of times. I shook myself awake, chiding myself to stay alert, but my earlier adrenaline rush had long since dissipated. I felt like a fool.

Of course it was too good to be true. There were no so-called allies, and my biological mother had no real desire to meet me. She'd probably died long ago and the messenger was every bit the liar Kole believed.

"She abandoned you," I whispered to myself, the sound jarring in the silence of the night. "She left you alone. Don't forget that."

So did Mom, a different voice whispered.

That particular thought was crueler than the rest, and it felt like a knife to the gut. But Mom thought she was helping us. It was the only reason she would . . . do what she did.

I sighed. Maybe I'd read the note wrong. If "where it all began" meant someplace else, the guy could be out there waiting for me, and I'd never know it. Perhaps if I returned home, there would be another note waiting.

"You showed."

I whirled around, aiming my stunner at the dark figure standing casually in the shadows. He looked amused by the weapon in my hands. I recognized his voice, but Kole hadn't let me see the guy that night, so this was my first look at him. Mid-twenties, perhaps, and either lanky or malnourished. The way he hunched over made him look even skinnier.

"Nice of you to waste half my night," I snapped. "I was about to leave."

"No, you weren't. Can we find somewhere farther from the street?"

"I don't think so. My driver wants to keep us in sight."

He smirked, and I mentally cursed myself for my inability to lie convincingly. Maybe Travers wouldn't have been a bad idea. And a few guards, besides.

"I'm unarmed," he said, "so you can put that thing down."

"Not yet. First, tell me why you burned my boyfriend's building down."

His twisted smile faded. "Sorry to disappoint, but that wasn't me."

I kept the stunner aimed at his chest. "And that wasn't you who met the Firebrand yesterday either, was it?"

Now he looked dumbfounded. "Wow, you people are paranoid. I did meet with one of them, actually. A lady who freaked me out a little. She wanted me to bring a message to someone."

"What did you tell her?"

"I said I would. Before you ask, it's on a chip, so I don't know what it says. But I don't think you need to worry anyway. Most people I know can't stand those guys. Whatever they want, they aren't likely to get it."

I nearly asked who the message was for, but I didn't want to derail the conversation. "You said you had some proof."

"Demanding one, aren't you?" He reached into his jacket and withdrew a piece of paper—not the kind from books but thicker. "Kadee Steer went back to the hospital to retrieve you when you were six days old. You were gone. The hospital refused to answer her questions and turned her away. She returned every day for a week until the administrator gave her this in secret."

I snatched it from his hand and angled it toward the streetlight. "Certificate of Adoption," it read. My parents' names were listed there, along with my name. There was no mention of a birth name or biological mother. The hope I'd allowed to flare inside me fizzled and went out, leaving my insides cold.

I shoved it back at him. "This isn't proof. There's nothing here that everybody doesn't already know."

"Look again." He pointed to the section with signatures.

I brought it closer to my face. There was my mother's signature—a butterfly with a square around it and her initials. And the strong hand of my father's signature—five hash marks crossed out to form a fancy *M* shaped like the Block. Beneath them, where it read "Biological Mother," someone had scrawled "Kadee Steer" in hesitant lettering. The "Father" line remained blank.

I handed it back to him, disappointed. "There is no Kadee Steer. My dad already searched years ago."

"That's because you searched NORA records."

I felt sick as the implication sunk in. "She's from Malrain."

"Bingo."

I had no idea what bingo meant, but I felt an odd dizziness join the nausea.

I carried Malrain blood.

Me, from the bloodthirsty nation that sheltered Virgil and sent soldiers to attack our borders. How many citizens had they killed over the last two decades? If my biological mother really was a foreigner, the mountain I climbed now had just gotten steeper. It would be hard enough to convince the country to allow the Hawkings' adopted child to rule, but a child of our worst enemy?

"Who was the father?" I asked numbly. *Please say he's from NORA.*

"That, you'll have to ask Kadee. She wants to meet you."

"Wait, you didn't say anything about me coming with you."

"Would you have met me here if I had?"

Not a chance. It didn't make me feel any better. I kept the weapon trained on him. "Why didn't she come herself?"

"She didn't have time. You'll see why soon enough."

"That's it?" I snorted. "You wave a certificate in my face and expect me to come with you, no questions asked?"

He sighed. "Look, you asked questions, and I answered them. If you want to know more, you'll have to come with me. We don't have much time. If we leave now, I can get you back by morning."

It was tempting. Oh, how I wanted to go with him. I imagined sitting at my biological mother's side and chatting about all the years we'd missed and the reasons she left that hospital without me and who my dad was. I wanted to see myself in her, to know I wasn't as alone as I felt and meet the extended family I never knew existed.

I wanted to escape all this. Just for a few hours, I wanted to set the name of Hawking aside and be myself. But that wasn't possible, no matter how badly I wanted it to be.

"I don't know how long you've been here," I began, "or how you even got past the border. But we're in the middle of a succession war here. I don't have one hour, let alone the entire night. If Kadee wants to meet me, she can sneak in however you did, and I'll do my best to meet her then."

He threw his head back and laughed. The sound echoed across the street, making me jump, but he didn't seem to care. "You think she wants a nice, cozy chat over tea? You really haven't heard of Kadee Steer?"

I gaped at him.

He chuckled again. This time there was a cruel tone to it. "You Hawkings are so oblivious. She's only the leader of the entire country, is all. It's an alliance she wants to discuss with you, not the weather. And she isn't even in

Malrain—she's hiding at our base a few hours away by train."

Had he just said . . . ? "Wait. You have a base within our borders?"

"You really need to get over the border thing. We've had people there for decades, since way before your group came. We've kept to ourselves ever since, so I'm not surprised you didn't know. Like I said, though, we have to leave right away if we're going to get you back by morning. You're the one who complained about being busy and all."

An alliance with Malrain. The words gripped my mind until I barely heard him. Dad and Gram would have spat at the very idea of allying ourselves with our enemies after years at war. But they weren't the ones fighting to save a country headed for disaster. I was. Visiting with Kadee wouldn't mean I agreed to anything. It was a meeting. Nothing more.

I thought about Kole and flinched. "I'm not going anywhere without a security team. We'll meet you here tomorrow night and go then."

He gave me a long look. "Do you really have time for that? I mean, don't get me wrong, but I thought your country was falling apart. And I think you'd have guards with you now if you thought I would hurt you."

I gripped the stunner more tightly in warning. "Who says I don't?"

He smirked again, but I fell silent. He was right about one thing—I *didn't* have time to wait. After the move to the island, traveling to the mainland would be much harder. After tonight, Kole wouldn't let me out of his sight. I imagined Kole sweeping through the house in a rage, looking for me and shouting at the guards, demanding to know where I'd gone. No, tomorrow wasn't really an option.

It was now or never.

"The slightest glimpse of danger and I'll use this thing," I told him.

"I have no doubt. You coasties have always been jumpy."

"*Coasties*?"

He shrugged. "You took the land along the coast and left us the driest parts."

"But still. That's a terrible word."

"If you say so." He smirked yet again, a look I was beginning to know well. Then he turned toward the train station and gestured for me to follow. "Okay, then, let's go."

SEVENTEEN
LEGACY

Chadd sat across from me, his knee bouncing impatiently in the empty aisle. Under the train's dim lighting, the shadow of growth on his chin and the redness of his eyes were easier to see. He carried no overnight bag. His shirt collar was opened low, showing very pronounced collarbones and a chain necklace. Around us, the seats were empty and smelled of sweaty shoes and old vomit. I doubted this train even ran this time of night. It must have cost Chadd a fortune.

I never thought my first train ride would happen quite like this.

I kept my stunner across my lap, watching his every movement. He seemed completely unaffected. Soon, he rested his head back against the seat and closed his eyes. When his mouth fell open and the sound of light snoring floated across the aisle, I let my attention drift to the window to watch the passing streetlights. I'd never been this far from home alone before, let alone with a stranger from Malrain.

"Out of range," the radio in my pocket alerted. "Out of

range."

I grabbed it and turned the dial, silencing the voice. I was officially on my own. An irrational joy welled up at the first real freedom I'd had in years. No official schedule, nobody questioning where I went or how I got there or why.

I'm going to see my birth mother. The thought sent a little thrill through me.

A woman's voice boomed in the speaker next to my head. "Northern border. End of the line."

I leapt to my feet, forgetting about the stunner in my lap. But I managed to catch it with one boot, softening its fall just before it clattered to the floor. I swept it up and swung back to Chadd, who watched me in amusement as the train began to slow.

"We're here, then?" I said, trying to look as unconcerned as he did.

"We have some walking to do, but yes." He rose to wait by the doors. They slid open with a whoosh. Then he leaped out and disappeared into the night.

I lingered, hiding behind the doorframe and squinting into the darkness. This was the moment of truth. The entire Malrain army could be out there, waiting for their prisoner to walk into their hands. For a second, I considered telling the train driver to close the doors and take me home.

A few seconds later, Chadd reappeared. "Coming, Hawking?"

I counted down, then leaped to the ground and took cover behind a bench. No shots came. Nothing moved in the shadows.

Chadd covered a smile. "Are you done?"

I glowered at him as I stood there. "I expected some kind of escort." Not the good kind either.

"Believe it or not, Kadee wants to keep this quiet as

much as you do. I'm taking you straight there myself. But we have to hurry. The train driver will only wait a few hours."

I fell in step behind him, following the outline of an old sidewalk, and tried to calm my pounding heart. This place felt . . . off. There was no grass, not a tree in sight, and the crickets were a distant memory. There was nothing but broken concrete and the remains of a train station lost to generations past. "Why did Kadee choose you?"

"I told you, she's my commander. I follow orders even when I don't understand their importance."

"You don't think this trip was important."

"Let's just say I don't think you're the solution to our problems. She disagrees."

"And the Firebrands? Are they the solution to your problems?"

"I highly doubt it. Be careful on these steps. There's a lot of debris." He started down a flight of stairs toward a mass of black in the distance. I shuddered to think what that blackness looked like in daylight and carefully picked my way down, grateful for the bright moonlight.

We walked in silence for at least thirty minutes before the city finally took shape around me. Or rather, what had once been a city. Now it looked like a massive pile of rubble against the distant blackness of the ocean. I hurried to keep up with Chadd, shuddering to think of the number of corpses a broken city this size could hide. It smelled of wet concrete and mud here, sending goose bumps across my skin. "The Old War?"

"Yep. Everyone died but us, as you'll soon see. If you stay on this path, it's easier." He motioned to a barely visible trail cutting through the debris and marched onward.

Soon he brought me to the remains of a storefront

missing its windows. This structure had survived better than its neighbors with their crumbling walls. Chadd didn't bother with the front door. He simply stepped over the window base and disappeared inside. I lifted my stunner as I followed, but there were only shadows. After letting my eyes adjust, I followed him toward the back. As we entered another doorway, the sudden brightness of golden lamplight stung my eyes. A flight of stairs descended into blackness.

"Don't trip," was all he said.

The air, thick and musty, somehow grew heavier as we descended. At the bottom, we turned into some kind of tunnel. I blinked. The walls were a patchwork of materials, mostly brick and mortar and old wood broken up by the occasional narrow door and support beam. Every few feet, an electric lamp lit the way. Not a tunnel, then. It almost looked like . . .

"The old underground city," Chadd said. "Long story. There was a big fire, and most of the city burned, and they wanted to fix some drainage issues anyway, so they set the new construction up a level. Eventually, the only businesses left down here were the rougher ones nobody wanted to see. Same with the people. When the war broke out, nobody remembered the outcasts below them until we were all that remained."

"You're descended from the survivors," I said breathlessly, taking it all in. "So you've lived here your whole life?"

"Until a few months ago. Kadee asked me to be a liaison for our people in the city. And before you ask, yes, we have hundreds of them throughout your country, and no, I'm not worried you'll root them out. You'd be surprised how easy it is for us to go unnoticed." He chuckled. "You don't even notice most of your own."

I frowned, but he plunged on.

"To answer your other question, there are more survivors than those you'll see down here. We have two other settlements, both larger than this one and situated along what you call the border. They used to be larger before your group came with their silent weapons and took our farms for their own. They even harvested the grain we planted."

Gram would never have allowed such a thing. I wondered if she even knew. "If that's true, I'm sorry. If I ever take the Copper Office back, I'll do my best to make it right."

He shrugged. "I think that's one reason Kadee wants to meet with you, to see if the call of your blood can drown out your upbringing." He motioned to the right, and we turned down another narrow hallway, then climbed a set of worn stairs. I still hadn't seen a single other person.

The call of my blood. Was that where all these doubts came from? After spending a lifetime hating Malrain because I'd been told to, I felt like the world had just been turned upside down. Walking around underground didn't help the sensation. "Where is everyone sleeping?"

"This is the historical district, where we do our business. We live in another section entirely, one they expanded before I was born. More natural light and better ventilation. You won't be seeing it, though, at least not until Kadee decides you can be trusted. It's already a huge risk for us to bring you here." His tone said it was a risk he didn't agree with.

It seemed an eternity before we reached another low, narrow door. This time, Chadd knocked six times and stood back to wait. A woman opened the door and narrowed her eyes at me. Her bleached-blonde hair hung long over her shoulders, tapering unevenly at the edges as if it hadn't seen a trim in years. Her hair nearly reached the old-fashioned pistol at her belt.

"Legacy Hawking to see Kadee, Aunt Rosa."

She stared me down in a silent warning before swinging the door wide. A torn black leather sofa sat against a wall covered in floral-patterned paper wilted at the edges. A desk, formed by two file cabinets and a long piece of thick glass, straddled the corner. A bright-red chair sat behind it. I felt like I'd entered an eclectic antique furniture shop the size of my closet at home. The heavy smell of dirt from earlier returned full force in such a small space.

"Just so we're clear," I told them both as I walked inside, "I'm not giving you my stunner."

"Leave it in your pocket, and we won't ask for it," the woman said. "Pull the trigger, and you won't leave this room alive. Sit." She motioned to the stool in front of the desk.

"I'd rather stand, thanks." I turned back to Chadd. "Where is she?"

"Coming." He situated himself next to his aunt against the wall, suddenly looking too much like a guard for comfort. Aunt Rosa continued to glare like I'd stolen her firstborn. Apparently not everyone was okay with my presence here.

"Aren't you going to tell Kadee I'm here?" I asked Chadd.

"She knows."

I stood there for a few minutes, feeling awkward, before finally sinking into the black sofa with the stunner across my thighs. My nerves felt like electric conductors sending a current of energy through my body. My mind kept sifting through all the reasons this meeting was a bad idea. Kadee could throw me into a dungeon somewhere, and nobody would know where I'd gone. I could end up dead, my body thrown in that massive pile of destruction above us, for the simple reason of who my parents were. I could be forced to agree to a treaty at knifepoint or get sick from some kind of plague. By the sound of tiny pattering feet, I knew the three of us weren't the only living beings in the room. There had to be thousands of rats down here, all carrying diseases from centuries ago. Yes, this decision could be very bad.

I didn't allow myself to follow that line of thought very far.

"You are a scientist," Rosa said, "like your mother, Andreah Hawking."

I lifted an eyebrow. She didn't seem like the chatty type. "Not exactly. I Declared—er, chose a position at Neuromen for personal reasons. I'll never be as smart as she was." Not like Millian and Kole and the lab assistants who slept in their new homes on the island right now.

"You wanted to find out who killed her."

I gasped, nearly throwing myself into a coughing fit. I kept forgetting how much these people knew about NORA —and how little I knew about them. "Yes, actually. But I know what really happened now."

"A shame she didn't remove her abomination of an invention from the world."

Chadd elbowed his aunt, who fell silent.

"No, you're right," I told her. "Virgil harmed a lot of people with her research. My mother never wanted it used in that way."

"I'm not so sure," Rosa spat.

"Aunt," Chadd muttered in warning.

I straightened in my seat, no small feat considering the depth of the cushions. "If you have a problem with me or my mom, I'm sorry. I hold no malice for any of you, but it's clear you can't say the same."

Rosa sniffed and turned her glare to Chadd. "I cannot stand here and pretend all is well when Andreah Hawking's daughter sits before me."

"Why?" I shot back. "My mom was a good person and a great scientist."

"She was neither. Good people don't hurt others, and when they do, good scientists don't cover it up. Andreah Hawking did both."

It took a second for understanding to dawn, and then I shot to my feet. "You were the assistant in that experiment, the one who got hurt. You disappeared because Virgil sent you here."

"I don't know who sent me," she hissed. "All I remember is pain like I've never felt before. It lasted an eternity. I thought I was dying. I woke up in a bed here a week later because Kadee found me dumped next to the train tracks. Even then I would have died if it weren't for Kadee's medicine."

My mind raced as I stood there, gaping at the woman, trying to piece the information together. Virgil had said Kole's torture was a new update "few" would get. He had seemed to already know what it would do despite the fact he'd never used it before—and he'd been fascinated by the process, almost like he'd wanted to do it to someone for a long time. What if he knew about it from Mom's research backup? The Neuromen custodian had mentioned Mom's failed experiment and a patient disappearing, but I'd assumed disappearing meant death. It never occurred to me to look for the woman here.

But it was her description of the experience that chilled me. I could almost picture it, almost see the woman on the floor, trembling in agony as every single nerve in her body fired at once.

Just like Kole.

"It was painful?" I asked with a small voice. "Did you have nightmares afterward, maybe throw things in your sleep?"

Rosa pressed her lips together, uncertainty reflecting in her dark eyes for the first time. "Nightmares, yes. And seizures. None of the healers could stop them until Kadee concocted a treatment that worked."

A treatment that worked. Excitement rose within me. "Do you think I could get—"

The wall behind the door slid open, and my biological mother entered.

EIGHTEEN

LEGACY

I TENSED as the door behind her slid closed without a touch. She stood there, looking me up and down with sharp eyes. Her brown trousers hung low on her narrow waist, held up by a thick belt, and a short black shirt clung tightly to her frame. A cloth headband the same red as her chair held her thick brown hair back.

But it wasn't her clothing that held me captivated. I could have been looking in a mirror. Besides her pale skin, she had my eyes, my slightly pointed chin, my slender neck sloping into narrow shoulders. She also looked about ten years younger than I'd imagined and was about my same height. She didn't look much like a commander, but there was no question we were related.

Chadd and Rosa straightened.

"Sit," Kadee said, sounding much like Rosa had.

Angling myself so I could keep an eye on all three at once, I sat on the stool in front of her desk as she took her own seat. "I'm Legacy Hawking." I paused. "Your daughter."

"Nobody else you could be." Her voice was clipped,

hard. There was no hint of a mother's warmth, no curiosity about my life. No indication that this woman wanted anything more of me than a midnight meeting.

I felt my cheeks warm. My dreams of a heartwarming embrace and tears and hours of reminiscing vanished into smoke. "Chadd said you wanted to discuss an alliance."

"Surely you have questions first. Even Chadd doesn't know everything."

The strangeness of it all pulled a bitter laugh from my lips. I'd left my home in the dead of night to come see the woman who'd given birth to me, yet she treated me like an annoying peasant complaining about bad crops.

"I have plenty of questions," I growled. "What I don't have is a lot of time. I'm trying to run a revolution."

"As am I. The fighting between our countries has taken far too many resources and needs to end. I understand you're dealing with a succession problem. Your brother, I believe?" Her eyes with knowledge. She knew far more than she let on.

Fine. Two could play that game. "My problem began with a scientist you gave asylum to recently. Tell me what you've done with Director Virgil."

"Ah yes. I've spoken with him on several occasions. Smart man. He's moved on, I'm afraid. Stayed with us for a few weeks and then left. I'm not sure where he ended up."

I watched her for a moment, trying to read her, but it was impossible to tell whether she told the truth. "He hurt a lot of people, and I think he's planning to do it again. If you can find out where he's gone, I would very much like to have him returned to us."

"I'll look into it." She cocked her head. "When you say he hurt a lot of people, I assume you refer to the brain chips, the ones that make it possible for your people to speak with each other wherever they are. Correct?"

"Implants, yes." I'd forgotten they didn't have the technology. Gram called people like Kadee vultures, and Virgil had mentioned something about Malrain wanting our tech, but I knew infuriatingly little about these people and their desires. "Virgil triggered an illness in some of our people."

"More than some, it seems. My sources say about 10 percent were adversely affected. Such a disaster. I wonder that you haven't leveled this mess to the ground and started over."

A chill gripped me. "Started over?"

"Well, the fires and the riots. Your medical system is in shambles, your brother seems nearly unglued, and your credit system has taken a dive. Workers aren't showing up for their jobs and are trying to switch to more secure ones under the radar, creating an illegal employment crisis. You need a clean start. New laws, a new cabinet. I can help you take what's yours. Align with me, and I'll solve your problems before week's end."

The implications began to sink in, and I shivered in the damp coolness of the underground. It wasn't an alliance Kadee wanted. She was asking us to step aside so she could attack NORA and put me on the throne. She wanted victory and everything that came with it—our technology, our resources, our military strength. Our land. And ultimately, an overhaul of everything that made my country what it was.

I imagined my followers, hungry and hopeful, watching me take the throne that way. They knew me as Legacy Hawking, not the daughter of a Malrain leader bent on winning at all costs. They would never understand. Gram would never understand. If Dad awoke, this would be the greatest betrayal of his life, and he knew what betrayal felt like more than anyone. Alex, if he survived the battle at all, would live the rest of his life convinced I'd sold the family out. He'd be right.

And Kole. After everything he'd sacrificed, winning this way would never feel like a victory.

I rose to my feet, cold disappointment ushering in a new level of exhaustion. "I shouldn't have come. Thank you for seeing me, but I can't agree to something like this."

A new hardness entered Kadee's eyes. "Like what? You would never have come if you weren't willing to negotiate."

If she'd asked me to meet her for the sake of beginning a relationship, I would have come for that alone. Clearly, the alliance meant more to her than I did. I was such an idiot. Nobody would ever replace Mom. How many times would I need to tell my heart that before it behaved as it should?

Kadee still watched me expectantly.

"I wanted you to loan us soldiers," I finally said. "We need to take the Block back and defeat the Firebrands. I can take it from there."

"How many soldiers?"

I blinked. She was actually considering this. "About four hundred, maybe five. But you'll never get there without being spotted far in advance."

She smirked, suddenly looking much like Chadd. "We'll get there just fine. But we're bound to lose dozens in this battle, so I'll need to be well compensated. I don't think my earlier demands were unreasonable."

"Giving you control over my country is *not* a reasonable demand."

Irritation flickered across her too-familiar features. "I could take NORA right now if I wanted. Your military is as scattered as your loyalties. But I have no desire to rule

NORA, and I'd rather put you on the throne than the alternative. We both want the same thing, Legacy Hawking—peace, stability, and prosperity. An alliance is how we get there."

My voice rose in pitch, incredulous now. "What you describe isn't an alliance. You can't really think I'd agree to let you attack us. People will die, and it will be my fault."

"People are dying anyway. We *will* defeat NORA, understand. I'm simply letting you dictate how and when. A true leader seizes the opportunity to benefit herself and minimize damages."

"Damages? Is that what you call it?" I snorted. "Forget it. I refuse to let you attack my people, now or ever. I can't believe you tricked me into coming here in the first place. You haven't said a word about the fact that I'm your biological daughter. No 'I'm proud of how far you've come' or 'I'm sorry for abandoning you in the hospital' or anything."

For the first time, a glint of uncertainty appeared in her eyes. "Did you expect that, Legacy Hawking?" she asked quietly.

"A little bit, yeah. I've wondered about you for years, yet you don't seem to care that I exist. At least you didn't until you discovered I could be used. But you know what?" I leaned forward, getting right in her face. "That's fine. The life I've led before now has been incredible, and every ounce of that is because of the Hawkings. I'll figure out how to get the Copper Office back without killing a bunch of my own people, and I'll do it without your help. I hope I never see you again." I stormed toward the door.

Her voice was even, unbothered. "Life has been far easier on you than it has on me, *daughter*. You know nothing of sacrifice. I suppose you don't even know the circumstances in which you came into the world, do you?"

"Why would I? You haven't told me a thing."

She motioned toward the stool I'd just vacated. This woman made the term *curt* seem long-winded. I glanced at Chadd and Rosa, but they didn't run to block my exit. They didn't even reach for hidden weapons. They just watched me curiously, as if interested in my response.

I'd come this far. May as well see it through. I retraced my steps to sit in the chair. "I have a few minutes. Do enlighten me."

Kadee placed her elbows on the desk, leaning closer to me. The hardness she'd displayed earlier turned hot and bitter. "I snuck into your city for a job that would support my two younger brothers after my parents died. One was six, one eight. They would live with a friend during my absence. Your hospital hired me as a janitor. Since I wasn't legal, they barely paid me anything. I slept in a custodial closet and used the physicians' showers after hours. My food was whatever the break room provided. It made it so I could send a little money home each month but barely enough for them to live on." Her voice lowered, and I saw the others lean forward as if straining to hear. "I fell in love with my manager, who kept my secret. At least I thought it was love. We spent several nights together sitting on the rooftop and talking. A few weeks later, I discovered you were coming. I was sixteen."

I felt a strangling sensation in my throat. *Sixteen.* Almost two years younger than I was now. No wonder she hadn't reported who my father was.

"I'm sorry," I told her, and I meant it.

She glanced at her hands, recovering quickly. "I didn't have the money for your birth, so a medic friend delivered you and helped me slip away. I returned home to find that my brothers had perished of disease months before and my friend had collected my payments for herself. I returned to my empty home and cried for two days. I decided I didn't want to be alone in the world anymore, so I went back to bring you home, but you were gone."

I swung one leg back and forth, letting the motion distract me from the horror rising in my chest. Not only was I the daughter of a single mother from Malrain, a girl who had only wanted me as a last-ditch alternative to a lifetime alone but also a man who had taken advantage of a minor—a man who probably still worked at the hospital right now. Kadee's hard manner hurt, but in a way, I understood how it felt to put up walls for protection. She'd lost everyone she loved too. We just handled our grief a little differently.

If I lost Dad and Kole both, would I end up as hardened and bitter as this woman? It was a question I couldn't answer.

One thing was clear. The life I now lived, as terrible as things stood, was a hundred times better than the one Malrain and Kadee would have offered. I tried to imagine being raised by this woman and her brusque manner, comparing her to my own mother, then gave it up immediately. It wasn't an image that deserved the validation of thought. My journey across the forest had been worth it for this moment alone.

Thank you, Mom, I thought, sending the words to the fates or wherever Mom lingered.

"The medicine you gave Rosa," I said. "I would like to buy some from you."

Beside me, Rosa went rigid. In a second, the vulnerability left Kadee's eyes and the Malrain commander returned. "Agree to my terms, and you'll have your medicine and my armies."

I swallowed, a new grief overcoming me. *Country before*

family. Country before self. No matter how much I cared for Kole, I couldn't sacrifice NORA to save him. Malrain mother or not, I was still a Hawking.

"Then we have no bargain," I said, "because I will never agree to those terms."

Kadee examined me for a long moment. Then she clasped her fingers together and leaned back in her chair. "You will change your mind, Legacy Hawking. And when the day comes that you must sacrifice your country to save your family, Chadd will be waiting—because Hawking or not, you're no better than the rest of us."

NINETEEN

KOLE

I LIFTED THE GLASS LID, inhaling the delicious aroma as steam rose to the ceiling. The rice inside was cooked perfectly—not like the crunchy type I'd grown up with, the old kind that never seemed to soften. I hurried to replace the lid so the steam wouldn't escape, then smoothed the tablecloth once again with a smile. This had to be the nicest meal I'd ever made, and I'd cooked it all myself. Never mind the fact that it had taken me three tries to get it right.

Darkness had descended an hour ago. The house around me stood silent, its earlier rush of boxes and people and noise gone for good, gone to "the island," a mysterious place everybody talked about but I'd never seen. Our last opportunity to be alone. Besides the guards hidden behind the bushes outside and on the rooftop, of course.

The first step in healing our relationship looked to have a promising start. I would finally tell her about the night-mares, maybe even the headaches. I wasn't ready for medical intervention, but maybe if I opened up about my problems, she would too. We'd be like a normal couple for a single night before jumping into battle again.

The smell of meat—real meat, not the canned kind—made my stomach rumble. Mom usually did the cooking for the three of us and, later, the two of us. When Mom got sick and I went to live with Dane, the fridge sat empty and the kitchen unused except as storage for his alcohol packets. So I'd begun to buy groceries and cook on my own. It wasn't great. I couldn't afford the synthetic meat offered at most stores in the Shadows, let alone real meat. But, occasionally, expiring canned meat went on sale. Paired with rotting vegetables and cheap boxed pasta, it made a decently nutritious meal I could make last a few days. At least when Dane didn't discover it.

But then Neuromen Labs happened, and then Legacy and me, and the past weeks had been spent scouring the streets for intelligence to keep her safe. I passed a credit here and there for cheap carbs, and it had worked fine. It felt great to prepare food again.

Despite the cook's protests, I'd managed to pluck a few ingredients and pans from the kitchen supplies this afternoon before the boxes reached the transport. This spread looked pretty decent, if I said so myself. A hashed meat in some kind of sweet sauce, white rice, and green peas I'd shelled myself. The only thing missing was my date.

I checked the watch on my wrist again, although it couldn't have been more than three minutes since I last checked, and frowned. Legacy had disappeared this evening during my trip to the store. A note on the table said she'd gone with the others to check on Millian and she'd be back tonight. I grabbed the radio in my pocket and stared at it, considering. Were Millian's injuries so extensive Legacy wanted to stay with her? I was woefully ignorant of girls and their friend relationships. I wasn't all that experienced in romantic relationships either, for that matter. Maybe

Legacy simply needed time with someone who wasn't a guy or family member. Maybe this whole thing was a bad idea.

I remembered my earlier conversation with Travers and slipped the radio back into my pocket. He was right. I trusted Legacy, but I hadn't shown her very well. Hounding her on the radio wouldn't exactly inspire confidence in that fact. *Ten minutes. I'll give her ten minutes.*

Ten minutes passed, then thirty. The pots holding the food went from hot to warm, then cool. The sounds of traffic outside quieted as families retired for the night. I stopped checking my watch after the second hour, worry rising within me. Maybe she'd fallen asleep at Millian's bedside. But that didn't sound right either, not with a team of guards standing around her. And she would have radioed me if she changed her mind about coming back.

I finally pulled out the radio and called her. The screen beeped. Out of range. I nearly threw the radio across the room, then tried again. And again. No luck.

By hour three, I'd tried at least thirty times. I finally radioed her assistant, Foster, and woke him up. He seemed confused by my question, insisting she had to be at the house with me because all guards were accounted for. I strode outside and yanked the guard captain from the bushes, asking whether they'd seen her leave. After a grumpy radio conversation, he admitted they hadn't.

The island thought Legacy was here. Everyone here thought she was on the island. That meant that either something had happened to her or she'd lied to everyone about her whereabouts. Something told me it was the latter.

My panic grew a hot edge of anger, like claws on a monster. The dull edges of another headache threatened an appearance. Maybe Travers was wrong. Maybe we were all deluded in thinking this relationship could work. I was tired of being lied to. My dad, Dane, Virgil, and now Legacy. We were supposed to be able to trust one another. How could I ever look her in the eyes again and truly believe she told the truth?

Once back inside, I grabbed the radio again and called Travers. When I told him the situation, he went quiet.

"Stay there," he said, his voice deep with concern. "I'll go looking for her. You have no transport, so you can't search very far, and it wouldn't do to have you captured by the Firebrands. If they get our new location out of you, we're all in trouble. It's possible she'll call you, so make yourself available and try to stay calm."

I growled in frustration. "Legacy is wandering the city alone in the middle of the night, and I'm supposed to stay calm?"

He paused. "I suppose that's an unreasonable request, but try anyway."

SEVERAL HOURS LATER, I considered tossing Travers's request out the window and running down every street in the city. I now knew the fireplace in the living room held eighty-two bricks—sixty red and twenty-two orange—and the floor 103 tiles. The back of the front door, a dark blue with peeling paint, had at least two layers of paint underneath it—a fiery red and a putrid dark purple barely visible in a chipped corner. By the state of the ceiling, this house had been built at least a hundred years before the Old War and only the kitchen had been updated since. I felt like a hound pacing a shelter cell, anger ticking upward with every minute Legacy spent out there alone after promising me she wouldn't.

I called Travers twice more until he finally responded, sounding exhausted. No sign of her. I tried Legacy's radio again and got the same message. Out of range. Where in this city could be out of range? Had she gone for a walk in the forest? A swim in the ocean? Or had someone found her and disabled the radio?

My feet ached from all the pacing, and my headache intensified by the hour. I sat at the table and buried my head in my arms, the food forgotten. My earlier anger had run its course, and a thousand scenarios ran through my mind, each more gruesome than the last. Legacy lying in an alley somewhere with her throat slit. Legacy's body rotting in a prison cell beneath the Block, hidden from the world. Legacy a splattered mess on a street somewhere, having been pushed off a building. Or maybe she stepped off herself. Travers and Gram had both said she suffered from the pressure. What kind of boyfriend was I if I hadn't seen any of it? Worse, I'd added to her stress with my own problems. Now I would never have the chance to tell her how sorry I was.

The front door opened with a long squeak.

Legacy peered inside.

TWENTY

LEGACY

Kole rose from his chair as I stepped inside. He'd moved the kitchen table to the living room and set out what looked like a nice spread of food and two place settings. Oh, *fates*.

"Did I forget about an anniversary?" I asked weakly, then mentally kicked myself. Of all the insensitive things to say after a night of lies. I closed the door behind me, half wishing I hadn't entered at all. The hurt and betrayal on Kole's face nearly sent me right back to that train and its end-of-the-line stop for good.

He didn't move, just stood there with his jaw clenched. "I wanted to surprise you."

"Consider me surprised. Did you cook?"

"I thought you were dead, Legacy. Travers has been searching for you all night. I was planning how to tell your grandmother."

A deep ache made me want to throw my arms around him, but the anger behind his eyes stopped me. "I . . . needed some time alone."

Kole looked like he'd been struck. "I get that you want to make your own choices. I really do. But don't lie to me."

I ducked my head, shame coursing through me. He had a right to be angry. We *had* agreed to stay together. But was it a lie when I only wanted to protect him from a hard truth? I'd taken a risk worth taking to secure victory for my country. I wanted them safe . . . but I also wanted Kole. I refused to believe I had to choose between them.

"Fine, I won't lie to you," I said, the exhaustion heavy in my voice. "But please respect that I can't tell you everything."

His eyes narrowed, and the hurt fled, replaced with a suspicion that immediately brought my guard up. "You owe Travers an explanation. You owe *me* an explanation."

"You'll get it, but not now. I'm tired. Let's discuss this later."

His voice shook with anger. "I don't know what you learned from that fancy tutor in that big house of yours, Legacy, but where I come from, we don't treat people like that."

"True," I shot back. "You just put their bodies in dumpsters."

He recoiled, shock spreading across his face.

I realized too late what I'd said. "Kole, I—that was uncalled for. I didn't mean you, just your kind in general. I'm tired. I wasn't even thinking—"

"No, you weren't." He strode toward me, his hand outstretched. I winced as he reached toward me, reminding myself he wouldn't hurt me. Not Kole, not ever . . . and then his hand brushed past me, gripping the door handle. He yanked on it and stalked out through the open door.

It took me a second to realize what was happening. "Wait! I didn't mean that. You need to believe me. We can fix this."

He halted just before the steps leading to the front yard. "I thought so, too, but after last night, I'm not so sure."

I glanced at the table again, taking in the meal he'd surely worked hard to prepare and realizing that he'd been up all night worrying. He cared about me. He wanted this to work as much as I did. That meant we still had a chance. "I want you to stay."

"And I want to be able to trust you."

"I want that too." I swallowed, feeling my life unraveling like string at my feet. I couldn't lose Kole. Not like this. "What would it take for you to trust me again?"

"Answers. Tell me where you were all night."

I bit my lip, watching him follow the motion. If I told him the truth right now, he would be less likely to trust me, not more. "Last night was a mistake. I'm not ready to talk about it yet."

His eyes went round in horror.

I realized what that sounded like. "No, no. I wasn't with a guy. I mean, I was, but it's not what you think. I knew he wasn't dangerous, and I was right, but I shouldn't have gone with him in the first place."

His expression grew darker by the second. "Chadd. It was Chadd, wasn't it? The guy I warned you had a meeting with the Firebrands the other day? The one who burned down my apartment building and *killed five families while they slept?*"

My face heated. "He said he didn't, and I believe him."

Kole stalked back inside, giving me barely a second to get out of the way before he slammed the door closed. Then he whirled on me. "Do you realize how stupid that was? And ditching your security team to go alone? You're lucky to be alive. Tell me where he took you."

I stared him down. "First tell me about your nightmares. The ones you keep insisting are no big deal."

He looked down at me with a murderous expression. *"Tell me where he took you!"*

Startled, I backed up and slammed into something hard, causing a rattling sound. A fork hit the ground. I'd nearly knocked over the table and its contents. "It wasn't Malrain, exactly," I stammered before I'd thought it through. "More like a settlement of theirs within our borders."

He roared, grabbed the chair beside me, and threw it over his head. It hit the brick fireplace and cracked clean in half.

"Kole!" I shouted, but then he turned on me, and I knew there wasn't much of Kole left in this monster. His eyes, a bloodshot red, were the eyes of a wild animal. He grabbed a pot and launched it across the room. It smashed into the front door, shattering the glass lid and sending a brown substance all over the room. I smelled a sweet sauce. Some kind of meat? My stomach sank even further.

"I told you!" he shouted, grabbing the table.

"Kole, no—"

He knocked it over, sending the other two pots to the floor, their lids clattering as the plates crashed down with them. Our romantic dinner lay spread across the room now.

Kole stood over his handiwork, heaving, looking like a victorious mountain bear. Amidst the rage in his expression was pain, as if something twisted a knife in his gut. He turned to me. I tried to step back but couldn't move, horror keeping me rooted in place.

Then his eyes rolled back into his head and he collapsed.

I stood there a second, staring at his limp form on the ground, disbelieving.

This couldn't be happening. Any second he would sit up, rise to his feet, and take me in his arms. But no matter how I willed it, his eyes remained closed.

It shook me back to my senses, and I fell to my knees next to him. "Kole."

No answer.

I cupped his face in my palm, then nearly dropped it in my shock. His skin was hot to the touch. *What in the fates?*

"Kole, wake up," I said in a shaky voice.

He didn't move.

I sucked in a ragged breath before remembering the radio in my pocket. I fumbled for it, yanked it out, and turned the dial to Travers's channel. "Travers? Are you there?"

A second later, his relieved voice answered. "Legacy. Where are you?"

"At the house."

"What's wrong?"

I choked back a sob. "It's Kole. I—I need a medic right away."

TWENTY-ONE

LEGACY

Travers and I dragged Kole upstairs to Dad's empty bed. I felt utterly exhausted by the time we got him situated, but I could do nothing more than pace the floor, waiting for Physician Redd to arrive. In the absence of the beeping medical equipment and oxygen tank, the room felt big and silent, the quiet nearly driving me mad.

Travers pulled a blanket over Kole, then adjusted it lower as Kole's face grew more flushed. My driver seemed to feel as helpless as I did. I recalled their whispered conversation yesterday and nearly asked what they'd discussed, but prying felt wrong with Kole lying there beyond my reach, hovering in the gray that bordered the darkness.

The physician arrived frazzled, his normally tidy hair in disarray. By the redness of his eyes and the crookedness of his collar, I could tell it had been a long night for him too. He and his medical team would have been setting up the new temporary hospital on the island and getting the comatose patients situated. I felt guilty pulling him away, but my desperation overshadowed everything else.

Kole had to be all right. I couldn't lose him now, not

when my country was falling apart around me and I'd rejected the very medicine that could have cured him.

Physician Redd rummaged through his hard-shell suitcase and retrieved a hand-held scanner, which he ran over Kole's head, first one way, then the other. A quick sweep of Kole's body took another minute. Then the man connected his scanner to a receiver of some kind and squinted at it for a long time. I watched with bated breath.

Finally, he replaced the device, closed the suitcase, and turned to me. That pain in my chest flared at his somber expression.

"I had hoped the damage would reverse itself," he said. The words he didn't say hung in the air between the three of us.

Kole was getting worse, just like Physician Redd warned.

"Perhaps if we'd put him under right away, we could have slowed the degeneration," he said. Physician-speak for *If you'd listened to me the first time, this wouldn't have happened.* But Kole had refused to even consider it, and I hadn't fought him very hard. I should have.

I should have stopped my mom. I should have saved my dad. I should have convinced Kole. I should have made the bargain with Kadee so I could bring the medicine back with me. I should have, should have, *should have* . . .

I didn't realize my cheeks were warm with tears until Travers put his arm around my shoulders. It was the most physical thing he'd ever done for me, and I gladly leaned into him as a second father. Not a replacement but a temporary substitute.

"He's dying," I said softly. The last word caught in my throat, coming out as a squeak. Travers squeezed me tighter.

"Not today, I would think," the physician said. "His

brain activity is already recovering—for now. But I recommend keeping him sedated, if not locked up somewhere safe. It won't be long before he has another attack, a worse one he might not survive. By the state of things downstairs, you're lucky to have survived this incident, too, Your Honor."

Travers looked down at me, his face drawn with worry.

"I'm not locking him up," I said firmly, avoiding Travers's gaze. "He would have hurt me by now if he could. Can you put him into a coma like Dad?"

Physician Redd sighed and closed his eyes. "The degeneration is too advanced. Your father has scarring on his brain like the burn left behind by a fire, which the brain *should* eventually repair on its own. Kole's damage is an imbalance of the body's natural electrical system. It quite literally needs to be rewired, something the medical community has never successfully done, although I've seen some promising research in the area of brain science. Much of it has come out of Neuromen, naturally."

Travers pursed his lips thoughtfully. "We retrieved everything we could from Neuromen and found no such research in Virgil's files. Even if it were hidden somewhere, the second fire at the warehouse would have taken care of what was left. I'm very sorry, Legacy. I feel somewhat responsible."

I barely heard him. A mantra ran through my head on repeat. *Heal Kole. Fix Dad. Save the country.* And now this new worry, with my biological-mother dictator who wanted to take over NORA. I rubbed my temples, feeling a headache coming on. "If—when—Kole wakes up, can we move him to the island?"

"He's safe to transport, but you don't have sufficient medical equipment there. If he has another attack, it'll take a hospital and a specialist to save him." Physician Redd hesitated. "Which leads me to an uncomfortable subject, Your Honor. Now that the lab on the island is running sufficiently, I'm afraid I have to step away."

I looked at him in surprise. "You aren't coming with us?"

He looked away and swallowed. I finally saw something in his eyes, something I'd noticed for days but hadn't wanted to consider. Guilt.

"Your patients aren't the only ones under my care," he said. "I have dozens of patients across town. I can't possibly abandon them."

His voice sounded hollow, much like mine when I lied. The realization hit me with the force of a slap. "You have a family. You're afraid."

His gaze snapped to mine. "My neighbor tried to join you and lost her home to fire, Your Honor. Her aged mother was lost. Thankfully, her children are all fine, but . . ." He trailed off.

I knew exactly what he meant to say. *I don't want my family to be next.*

"But we still need to figure out how to safely remove the implants," I told him. "Until Millian discovers how to get our comatose patients to heal, the entire country is vulnerable to future attacks. We're counting on you."

The words only seemed to deflate him. "I've done everything I can do. It's up to Millian now. If anyone can unlock the secrets of the brain and the implant, it's her. I've never had such a brilliant assistant."

I wanted to grab his shoulders and shake him. Millian couldn't solve anything from a hospital bed. But he'd already made up his mind. I knew what it looked like to give up, and Physician Redd had.

"I understand," I said, feeling limp with resignation. I didn't just fight against my brother and his minions these days. I also fought between fear and love and loyalty and confusion. *Country before family. Country before self.* The Hawking family creed wasn't for everyone, and I certainly wouldn't be forcing it upon my followers. I thought about the sleep this man had missed over the past weeks and the risks he'd taken, and swallowed the rest of my objections.

"I hope you win, Your Honor. I truly do." He paused. "Take care of him. He has two broken ribs."

I stiffened. That hadn't happened tonight, which meant I wasn't the only one keeping secrets. We truly were broken. "Thank you."

He nodded, silently gathered his belongings, and left.

Travers and I sat in silence at Kole's bedside for a moment before Travers spoke. "I'd be incredibly grateful to know what happened, Miss Hawking."

The truth burned in my throat, desperate for escape, and then it all came rushing out in a series of bursts and sobs. My driver held me through all of it. I even told him about my biological mother and her "offer." He stiffened at that but didn't say a word until I finished. In fact, he didn't say a word for a very long time.

It was I who broke the silence. "I don't know what to do. I want to beat Alex, but . . ."

"Not by recruiting your enemies to help," he finished for me. "And now you've paid a heavy price for that visit last night, possibly bringing on a Malrain attack you didn't expect and triggering an episode in the man you love—an episode that could divide you forever, both emotionally and physically. Is that a sufficient summary of your thoughts?"

I stared at him. "Actually, yes."

"I thought so. My own thoughts have yet to sort themselves out, I'm afraid, but I do know one thing. You can barely stand upright. I insist you use the bed down the hall and give your mind a rest. I'll watch over you and Kole until it's time to travel. Solutions rarely present themselves to minds that can't function properly."

I looked at him in wonder, suddenly seeing Travers in a new light. His sacrifices over the past weeks came to mind—the boat drives, the transport chase, the cell under the Block, the wife he'd lost. I owed my life to him several times over.

"I lied to you about where I would be last night," I told him, "yet you're still here. Why?"

His eyes crinkled around the edges as his mouth formed a tight smile. "I didn't have to become your driver, Legacy Hawking. Your father gave me a choice. It's something I've never forgotten, and I . . . I want that freedom for everyone else. Every member of this country deserves that much. It's you who will give that to them." A note of deep sorrow filled his voice. I wondered if he thought about his wife. "Now, go, or I'll shove you out myself."

TWENTY-TWO

LEGACY

TRAVERS WAS RIGHT. By the time I awoke to voices floating up from downstairs, I felt much better. I could almost pretend that things would work out—that my dad would awaken soon, that my followers were safe, that Kole slept in his apartment across town, stubborn and healthy, and that our victory was certain.

Kole.

I hurried to his room, anxiety gripping my heart. But I halted just inside. It wasn't Travers who sat at Kole's bedside.

"Millian!" I shrieked and threw my arms around her. I hadn't seen her awake yet.

"Hurt . . . ouchie . . ." she moaned.

I released her with a sheepish grin. "Sorry. I forgot."

"You do that a lot."

"Forget, or apologize?"

"Both," she said with a wink. I stood there for an awkward second or two, relieved to see her so well after a night in the hospital. She moved more slowly now, as would be expected from a stunner bruise to the chest and a concussion. A few small scratches marred her deep-brown skin, and the corner of a white bandage peered over her neckline. But there was defiance in her dark eyes, and she'd taken the time to pull her hair up into a huge black bun on top of her head. A good sign.

"Stop gawking and pull up a chair," she said. "I'm fine, and so are the lab assistants, minus the four who went into hero mode. The lab not so much, but we'll deal with that. So, what did I miss? Kole felt left out and wanted some attention from his girlfriend for once?"

The gravity of Kole's condition hit me again. I felt my smile fade as I plopped onto the floor by her feet. "Something like that." Kole looked the same as before, slightly flushed and too still. I took his hand, grateful for the warmth of his fingers, however limp they were.

"I saw his file." Millian shook her head. "I hate saying this, but he needs a solution we don't have—right now, anyway."

I knew it was true, but hearing Millian say it felt like a closing door. Millian, the eternal optimist, didn't give up unless something was a lost cause. I swallowed hard and tried to change the subject. "Well, now we have no head physician, no lab, and none of your research on the others. We have to start all over again."

Millian looked at me sheepishly. "Some of that isn't exactly true."

Wait. "Which part?"

"Pretty much the whole thing. I've already promoted one of the medics to head physician, and we've started putting together a new lab on the island. The hotel already had a small medical room, so that worked perfectly. But that isn't what I came to tell you. Are you ready for this?" She leaned over to look me straight in the eyes. "I know how to heal the affected patients. Legacy, I know how to heal your dad."

MILLIAN TOLD me all about it on the way to the island. We sat in the back seat, Millian supporting Kole's legs while I cradled his head in my lap. He felt a little cooler now. I hoped that meant he would wake up soon. My head still whirled with the sudden surge of hope churning alongside my usual dread, and my body buzzed with adrenaline.

Dad would be okay. He really would. It felt like someone had just told me fairylands and unicorns existed.

"Okay, you've explained it to me twice, but I still don't get it," I told Millian. "Can you cut the science-y words and pretend I'm five, please?"

"Come on. Even five-year-olds would have picked it up by now."

My heart pounded so hard it was entirely possible Millian was right. But I hadn't allowed myself to hope in so long. It felt like my brain teetered at the edge of insanity and unconsciousness and Millian was the lone tether that rooted me to the ground. "Just try. Please?"

She seemed to understand. "Fine. It was Physician Redd who gave me the idea. He made a note in Kole's file about needing his brain rewired or something, which is obviously impossible because the brain doesn't have wires. It has neurons, and neurons are built to repair themselves unless something prevents that, as we discussed the other day. Then I remembered we *do* have wires, tiny ones in the implant chips. Yanking the entire chip out is a huge shock to the system and can send someone into cardiac arrest, but if you go into the chip itself and disconnect each wire, one by one, leaving the chip in place . . ."

"It's permanently disabled," I breathed. "You're a genius."

"I know. You totally owe me. The new head I just appointed is already prepping a few of the failing patients for surgery. It's worked on one person so far, a councilman whose readings improved even before we closed him up. It may take some therapy to encourage healing, but if his scans continue to look good, I think we can wake him up in a few days."

I didn't bother to push down the thrill rising in my chest. I could have Dad back a couple of months from now. It didn't change everything else that hung over me, but it made it a little lighter somehow. "Thank you."

"Of course. I just wish that would help Kole. His case is so unique. It doesn't help that he's the only one Virgil tested his torture update on."

Torture update.

Understanding slammed into my brain so hard I thought for a moment that the Firebrands had struck me with their cannon. I gasped.

"Whoa, what's the matter? Legacy?"

I looked at Millian, but I didn't really see her. All I saw was Kole a few months ago, groaning as if about to be crushed by an incredible weight, his veins bulging as his face turned a deep purple. No wonder Mom had been so horrified by her experiment, so guilty. No wonder she wanted to take that research out of Virgil's hands. She knew what he could do with it.

With power like that, he could take out the world's leaders and place himself in charge instead.

"Whoever controls the IM-NET controls the world," he'd once told me.

It all made sense now. Since people no longer trusted their implants, Virgil needed something else to control people—a required device placed near the brain, seemingly harmless, where his updates could still take effect when he wanted them to. The people of NORA would never accept Alex's mandated implants after what happened. They were too smart. But half the country supported Alex and the Rating system, which meant they would accept the number screen in their foreheads without question.

They wouldn't know or even care that the two technologies came from the same source.

"Kole isn't the first," I finally said. "There's someone else who's been through this and survived. I learned about her from a janitor at Neuromen, and I think I may have found her among the Malrain last night. But the medicine she used is impossible to get."

"Nothing is impossible. Hard, maybe." She snorted. "I'm a dark girl from the Shadows, and I made it to Neuromen, so I know a thing or two about hard versus impossible."

I looked at her in surprise. "I thought you grew up in the upper district."

"Because I'm smart, right? And only rich people can be articulate and intelligent. I've heard it all before. If I have any success, it's because of my parents, my family, my school. Not me." She chuckled bitterly. "Nobody will ever know the truth about how my dad got hurt at work and they stopped paying him till he recovered. He couldn't transfer or complain to anyone or he'd get demoted for good, so he left us. Nobody knew about my mom's nightly visitors after that or how they started asking for my older sister too so we'd hide in my closet all night long, afraid to sleep. My sister said she wanted to run away, but she didn't want to leave me alone with *them* and I refused to leave Mom, so she stayed. Nobody knows about the evenings Mom spent weeping in the pantry or the treats she left on my bed when I did well on exams. They both said I was the one who would save them, that my brain would pull us all out someday."

"Oh, Millian." I took her hand, stunned and horrified. How had I not known any of this?

She didn't pull her hand away. Instead, she turned toward the window. "And then my sister got sick and we couldn't afford a medic, much less a hospital stay. I was so excited when I got the invitation to Neuromen." She paused, looking a little lost.

"And then it burned down," I finished for her. I'd set that fire. Me, so determined to save the world I hadn't thought much about the individuals in it. It hadn't occurred to me that Millian's helping me destroy Virgil's plans would also destroy her own.

My friend shook herself back to the present, her voice firm once again. "She still isn't doing well. Physician Redd was supposed to take a look when we got settled, but now . . ."

She didn't have to say it. He was gone for good.

"You just remember one thing, Legacy Hawking," she finally said, turning to face me, her voice fierce. You aren't the only person with someone to lose."

I felt sick. I'd never understood what went on in her life, and that wasn't her fault. It was mine. Irrevocably, irretrievably mine. I threw my arms around her neck and pulled her close. "I am *so* sorry," I whispered. In all my pain, I hadn't been able to see hers. I'd overlooked Travers and made Kole worry and assumed Millian worked hard for her own ambitions when her stakes were far higher than I knew.

"You like to think you're alone in this," Millian said against my ear, "and you have to save the country by yourself. Do you realize how insulting that is? We're all making sacrifices. Don't throw ours away in pursuit of yours. I care about Kole, too, but his isn't the only life at stake. This war is about all of us."

Her words healed something in my soul. With a friend like Millian, I finally had a chance. Dad would be fine soon, we would help the comatose patients recover and return them to their families, and word about our success would spread. Once my supporters were all settled on the island, we could revisit the announcement about the Ratings idea and convince the country to side with me. After that, anyone supporting Alex would seem like a fool. One step at a time, we could actually do this. For the first time in weeks, I saw a real future for all of us.

"I have been a little ridiculous, haven't I?" I asked sheepishly.

Millian grinned and pulled away, straightening in her harness. "That's a good start, Your Honorable Legacy Hawking-ness. We may have hope for you yet."

THE DISORIENTATION of waking up lasted a full minute. I tossed the wool blanket aside and instantly felt a chill in the air. I swung my feet to the floor, taking in the strange details—a curved concrete ceiling, a cold floor with a drain in the center, and one dim lamp across the room. No windows. No watch on my wrist, either. Day or night? I couldn't tell.

Muffled voices sounded through the wall. The door sat open a few inches, revealing a dark hallway. I stood up, steadying myself on the wall as my head spun, and peered out. Nobody in sight. This was no ordinary building. The island? If anything, we had to be underground.

The scurrying of rat feet followed me as I searched for the voices. They grew louder as I approached a closed door. One voice was distinctly Legacy's.

I yanked the door open, and five sets of eyes turned to stare at me. Nearly every available inch of the small space was filled. Legacy sat in a chair against the far wall, Gram at her side, Travers next to the door, and some man and a redheaded woman next to Travers. They hadn't even been given a seat. There wasn't room. The redhead's eyes drifted down to my bare feet.

I rested against the doorway. "Please continue."

"Kole," Legacy said, her beautiful eyes all lit up. She stood as if to run to me, then seemed to think better of it. "I'm glad you're up."

"We're on the island," I said matter-of-factly. I could smell the salty ocean in the air along with the cold, wet concrete surrounding us.

"Yes." Legacy shifted her feet, looking uncomfortable— about the watching eyes of others or my presence here? "This section is an offshoot of the underwater tunnel. We found it gives us more privacy than the resort. How are you feeling?"

The dizziness and fog of confusion had begun to clear, making room for my memories to return. Then they returned all at once—a tidal wave of light and color. Counting floor tiles. Out of range. Plates crashing. A table on the ground. Legacy flinching as I yelled at her, wanting to hurt her like she'd hurt me, and the exhaustion and terror and emotion taking over. And behind it all, a massive headache that nearly blinded me.

I gasped.

Legacy took a few steps forward, fear in her eyes. "Maybe you'd better go lie down."

The tidal wave dissipated, and I found myself standing in the doorway again, staring at five anxious faces.

I cleared my throat. "How long have I been out?"

Legacy continued to stare at me like I'd sprouted a tail.

"Two days," Travers answered for her. "I'll go find a medic."

"No," I said quickly. "That can wait until after the meeting. Don't stop on my account."

"Aren't you that Firebrand?" the balding man said. It wasn't accusing. More like annoyed.

I looked him dead in the eye. "Not anymore. You know what, Legacy? It's a little stuffy in here. I'll be your doorstop for a while."

Gram coughed to hide a smile. Travers didn't bother to hide his own.

"Okay," Legacy said. She swept the room one more time as if trying to fit me in somewhere, then seemed to give up and found her seat again. "As I said, we'll have to excuse Millian. She's prepping the medical facilities for the procedure. She did request that the ventilation team make the operating room their priority. We need it sterile enough to begin the first surgery this afternoon. Councilman Barber, can you make that happen?"

"I don't think—" the man began.

"Sure he can," Gram interrupted. "Now, let's get on to your biggest news. You mentioned the Rating system?"

Legacy's eyes flicked to me, hovered for a second, then returned to the others. "I think I know what Virgil is planning to do. When he launched the last update and targeted most of our leaders and wealthier citizens, I told him he wouldn't get away with it. Everyone would connect their loved ones' illnesses to the update and distrust it from then on. He said he expected that and went on about NORA being an experiment and Virgil's tech opening doors for him. I didn't think much about it. Then the Firebrands began secretly implanting the homeless with Rating screens and triggering some kind of torture, the same thing Kole went through." She paused. "I think Virgil knew we would eventually learn how to disconnect our implants. That's where the Rating screens come in. He's pushing Alex to implement them as a replacement for the brain implants."

"So he can target his enemies again and place his people in power," Gram said flatly.

"I think it's even worse than that," Legacy said. "Once NORA is under his control, he means to use our entire country as an experiment. He'll work out any issues with the tech on our citizens, then offer it to other countries. Soon the rest of the world will embrace the Rating system and its dangerous tech right along with it. Because of Virgil, every country's leaders will be able to torture their enemies or citizens into submission at the push of a button. He'll be the richest man in the world."

"Holy fates above," the woman across the room whispered.

I pressed my lips together, knowing Legacy was right. As a Firebrand, I'd seen the Rating system as an inevitable shift of power—less control for the powerful, more for the powerless. At least, that's what Dane had promised if we succeeded. Was that what he'd promised Dane to help him bring all this about? Had Virgil offered Dane and Alex a country in exchange for the world?

"That seems like a stretch," Councilman Barber said, the corner of his mouth tugging into a smile. "At best, this is a wild theory. You can't possibly think the entire globe is at risk, Your Honor."

Legacy and Travers exchanged a look. "I have reason to believe Virgil has already struck a bargain with Malrain," she said.

Her little jaunt into enemy territory with that Chadd guy. I struggled to hold back the low hum of anger that sprang to life inside me. Now wasn't the time for that particular argument. As betrayed as I felt by Legacy's choices, I wouldn't undermine her authority here. She glanced at me again as the room settled into an uncomfortable silence and everyone contemplated what this meant for our little movement.

Her theory did sound a little far-fetched, or at least it would have if I didn't know Virgil. But I did. Legacy and I knew better than most what the man was capable of, and I had to agree that Legacy had it exactly right. We'd been so busy fighting the immediate threat we hadn't seen the real threat creeping up on us from a distance.

"I still don't understand this torture thing," the redhead —Councilwoman Marium?—said thoughtfully. "How does it work? Virgil pushes a button and his implant zaps people? But the Rating screens don't work that way."

"I can answer that." Gram spoke with a glint of anger in her eyes. "In my day, the Rating system required two technologies—the implant screen in the forehead and the techband. When you tried to remove one, the other triggered punishment mode. It essentially electrocuted the victim. This sounds like a more chilling version of the same concept."

Councilwoman Marium shivered. Everyone else looked worn down, defeated almost.

"Let me get this straight," I said. "It's your brother Alex, the Firebrands, Virgil, *and* Malrain against the people in this room and the supporters above us. And everything hangs on whether the Rating system is implemented here in NORA. So we need to make sure everyone knows what Virgil plans to do with the Rating system, right? Then the citizens of NORA will rise up against it."

"Yes and no," Gram said. "The Rating system brings all the things you used to want, Firebrand. It's simple—put a screen in your forehead and get medical care for your sick daughter you couldn't afford before. Don't put up a fight, and your financial situation immediately improves.

Virgil is a smart man. Mark my words. He'll offer the country a new system of government that addresses the citizens' concerns and the Rating system as the means to deliver it."

"But if we make an announcement as we originally planned, it'll be our word against theirs," Legacy said.

Councilman Barber snickered. "The word of a group of rebels against the word of NORA's legitimate heir and leader of the country? That doesn't seem problematic at all."

"There's one other problem," Councilwoman Marium said. "We put a team outside three different stations, and none of them have sent reporters out in the past few days. Rumors say Alex changed the Right to Information laws. Stations must now submit their reports to the Copper Office for authorization or they get shut down."

Gram sat up straight in her chair, nearly throwing her lap blanket to the floor. "He can't do that!"

"Your Honor!" Legacy's assistant ran up, his face red with exertion. "His Hon—uh, your brother is making a speech. It's a mandatory broadcast. You can view it in the mechanical room."

Everyone in the room looked at each other, then leaped to their feet. I moved aside as they shoved their way out the door, Gram right in their midst. The woman had elbows. Then Legacy and I were alone.

She stopped in front of me, her eyes locked on mine. "You came back to me," she said softly.

"Did I hurt you?" I asked, my voice tight.

"No."

Thank the fates. "But I scared you."

"Yes." She didn't back down in the slightest. "You aren't well, Kole."

I looked back at the doorway, but the others were long gone. "I know."

"It's your brain, not you. Don't ever think there's something wrong with you. Okay? We'll figure this out. We'll stop it from happening again, and we'll get you medicine that will fix it. I haven't figured out how yet, but—"

"Legacy," I interrupted.

"—always a way. We have to believe that. We're going to beat this."

"*Legacy.*"

"What?"

I smiled wryly and lifted one hand to her cheek. To my relief, she leaned into my touch. "You're the most captivating and infuriating girl I've ever met. You're stubborn, impulsive, and a little . . . *Hawking* at times. I still can't believe you went alone with him."

She gave me a self-deprecating smile.

"You're all of that and more, but I knew all those things when this started. I knew it the first time I saw you walking down the halls at school, your chin held high as you stared down anyone who questioned your right to be there. I knew it that last day you blocked the doorway and refused to move even for a Firebrand. And now that I know you even better, I'm still here. Don't you get it? I'm not going anywhere, no matter what the physician or specialist or anybody else says. I guess what I'm saying is, if you want to make this work, I'm willing."

She closed her eyes against my touch, letting me cup her face in my hand. "I want that more than almost anything."

I gave her a sideways look. "Almost?"

"Well, it would be nice if my dad lived and the world didn't end because we failed."

Now I understood. "And you got the Copper Office back."

She shook her head. "Nope. That's third."

I had no doubt she meant it, and it made me love her more than ever. It was nice to stand here alone, separated from the world through several meters of concrete and kilometers of water and pretend we were a normal couple. She seemed to feel it, too, because she looked more relaxed and happy than I'd seen her in a while.

I motioned to the ceiling. "How's the island? Do you think I'll like it?"

"That depends." She bit her lip. "Do you like llamas?"

I laughed and brought my other hand to her face, stroking my thumb across her cheek. Her eyelashes fluttered as she stared at my mouth, awakening something inside me. I lifted her chin upward and leaned in before remembering. "Oh. The broadcast. We'd better get over there and see what Alex is saying."

She grimaced. "They'll be recording it, and I already know what he's going to say. Saving the world can wait two minutes."

"But—"

She placed a finger on my lips, then pulled them down to hers.

TWENTY-FOUR

LEGACY

WHEN WE ARRIVED at the mechanical room down the corridor, my hand tucked safely inside Kole's, it wasn't Alex's face that filled the screen. It was Virgil's. His time in Malrain had changed him. There was a tightness to his eyes that hadn't been there weeks before, and beads of sweat were visible on the very top of his bare head. Above all, he sported a new discoloration in his skin that looked like burn scars. In the background stood part of Neuromen that hadn't been destroyed in the fire.

He was back.

"What did I miss?" I asked the others, who stood at the rail behind a row of seats filled with technicians intercepting the broadcast. The earlier dread settled onto my shoulders again, but with Kole at my side, it didn't feel quite so daunting.

"Your brother announced that NORA's relay stations have all been taken back," Foster said, frowning at the screen. "And that you and your supporters been driven out for good. He said the fires are likely to stop now, but he's increasing patrols just in case."

Kole swore. A few choice words of my own came to mind, but I felt too glum to voice them. Of course Alex would blame the fires on us.

Millian ran into the room, breathless. She wore scrubs and a surgical mask slung over one ear. She glared at the screen. "I heard. Had to see it for myself."

Foster stepped aside, making space for her. Then he began to fill her in, leaning close to whisper. The tips of his ears turned pink as he did.

Virgil continued. "It's clear now that the system of government established under Her Honorable Treena Hawking was a rudimentary one at best. We've tried adapting it, but if you'll excuse the expression, placing a pretty hat on roadkill doesn't change the fact that it's roadkill."

Gram sniffed loudly. If Virgil were here, he'd have a palm mark on his face right now.

"The uncertainty of these past weeks has shown us more than ever that change is needed," Virgil said. "Our current system isn't adequate to support a growing, maturing nation. After conferring with experts and specialists in the areas of economics, science, politics, and sociology, His Honor and I have come to a decision. Neuromen will no longer be a science and technology lab. New construction has already begun to repurpose my lab into something far more important—the first Rating control center for our new system."

"I knew it," Millian said. "You called it, too, Legacy."

I only nodded. It gave me no pleasure to be right about this.

Virgil droned on in his artificially somber tone. "You'll recall that the original Rating system was an imperfect one. This modified version will be better, cleaner, and give you more freedom than ever before. You'll recall that some citizens were given priority over others when our last medical emergency occurred. Now, priority will be given to those who have earned it rather than those born with privilege and power. In time, we'll be stronger than ever—and your loved ones will finally be taken care of. The perfect system at last." He smiled.

"I might just murder that man," Gram muttered.

Travers glowered at the screen. "I'll drive you over, Your Honor."

Virgil's smile brightened. "And, now, for the best news of all. You'll recall my absence the past few weeks. I'm pleased to announce that I have not only recovered our previous technology but improved it. Our Honorable Alexandrite Hawking demands perfection from this new system as we end the dark days of inequality, and we've given him nothing less. It's my pleasure to announce that locations for Rating implantation will open in just two days. You will receive a message via your brain implants regarding your date, time, and location. Employers will be notified and your absence excused without penalty. In the meantime, be patient as we emerge from these hard times into a more bright and glorious future. May New NORA forever prosper." The screen went dark.

"Two *days*?" Millian exclaimed. "How can they possibly have the materials they need for distribution already? We were supposed to have weeks to fight this."

Gram frowned. "The materials should have taken months to manufacture and ship. If he has them already, he got them from someone who already had them. But who?"

"Kadee Steer," I said bitterly. "Malrain's leader." Not only had she lied to me about her intentions, she'd made it sound like a bargain was a possibility, which couldn't be true if she and Virgil already had an agreement. No doubt Chadd had burrowed himself in the city to help with transactions just like this—smuggling his own people in and out, transporting illegal products like Rating screens. They probably even used that night train. No wonder Chadd had been so casual about my presence and receiving messages from Firebrands. Kadee and her people dealt with whoever would give them what they wanted. They had no true loyalties to anyone from NORA, Malrain blood or not.

I'd been so naïve.

"We have to stop those implantations," Gram said. "As soon as they begin, we've failed. I won't have such an abomination occurring in this country while I draw breath."

To my surprise, it was Millian who patted her arm. "We can stop this, Your Honor. People have to be concerned right now. There will be protests, maybe even riots. We'll figure out a way to get the word out, even if we have to hijack a news station to do it."

Foster laughed. "A news station. Good one."

Millian gave him a cross look. "I'm serious."

"Oh, okay," he said a little too quickly. "Sorry. Um, what did you have in mind?"

While they began to whisper between themselves, Gram listening intently with a frown, I looked around the room at my closest friends and political allies, and two truths began to settle deep within my soul.

First, we were losing. It turned my thoughts bitter to even consider that, but I couldn't deny it any longer. It would take a brutal change of course to turn the tide of this war, and no video broadcast could do that. I thought again of Physician Redd's guilty look as he admitted his fears. He'd be far from the only one who felt that way.

Second, I had to find out the details of Kadee's deal with

Virgil and, by extension, the details of her bargain with Alex and the Firebrands. All I could see were bits and pieces of the full picture. Without all the information, we couldn't possibly fight this.

"Foster," I said. My assistant jerked his head up and hurried over. "Some of my supporters aboveground will have seen that broadcast. Everyone will be worried. Tell them we have a plan. We won't let them be forced into Ratings or anything else. Tell them to stand by."

His eyebrows shot up. "We have a plan?"

"The beginnings of one. Just tell them, okay?"

He nodded. I stepped into the hallway and headed down the corridor toward the stairs, deep in thought.

I hadn't yet turned the corner into the stairwell when Kole caught up to me. "Why do I have the feeling you're going to disappear again?"

With a sigh, I turned back to him. He would never agree to my plan. It would have been easier to sneak away and get it done than get permission. But something stopped me from telling the lie that sprang instantly to mind. Instead, I decided to trust him—and by extension, allow him to trust me.

I chose to try.

"There's something I have to take care of," I told him, "and I need your help."

Relief spread across his face. "Tell me what I can do."

TWENTY-FIVE

LEGACY

Chadd didn't show at midnight, nor half past. I found myself half relieved he hadn't come and half worried he never would. The rest of my cabinet would have found my plan "reckless" and "impulsive" anyway, plus all the other words that could be summed up in the term "too inexperienced to hold office." But tonight I didn't care. Virgil had made his move, and we didn't have time to argue about it. It was time to cut Virgil's nicely laid plans to pieces, one by one.

Kole shifted in his stance often as we waited, his eyes darting from one shadow to the next. I saw none of Monster Kole in him tonight. Occasionally, he left my side to investigate a sound or check the bushes and trees around us, but the rest of the time, he stood against me, making me aware of little else but the hardness of his arms, the gentle rising and falling of his ribs against my side, and his quiet exhale in the chilled air.

As he watched the shadows, I stared up at the tall, dark hospital looming above us. I'd come into the world in that building. I existed because of a young girl's loneliness and an evil man's lust. Part of me wanted to march inside, track my biological father down, and drag him to a prison cell. But I wouldn't be able to identify him without Kadee, and I was in no position to demand DNA testing just now.

Later, I promised. Whether I liked Kadee or not, no sixteen-year-old orphan deserved to be treated like that.

"How do you know he'll come?" Kole grumbled at one o'clock.

"He'll have people watching. They'll alert him that we're here."

"That isn't comforting."

I scanned the shadows, which moved ever so slightly, like tree limbs in the breeze, and shrugged. "They would have attacked by now if they were going to."

"That's not comforting either." He stepped closer to me, but he didn't demand we leave.

About two hours after midnight, a skinny figure strode up the lawn and planted himself in front of us. He wore all black and an expression that said, *You'd better not be wasting my time.* Kole aimed his stunner at him, looking every bit the trigger-happy guard.

"I don't have time to go to Malrain," I told Chadd. "But I want to talk to Kadee. I know you can communicate with her because she expected us the first time, so don't lie to me."

His mouth opened like he'd meant to do just that. I could see the guy recalculating. "Uh, why don't you give me the message, and I'll pass it to her."

"Not good enough," I said. "Get her on your device now. I want to talk directly to her."

"But—"

"The lady said now," Kole growled, sticking the stunner in Chadd's face.

The guy looked back and forth between us, then gave a long sigh that sounded more like a groan. I heard the protest of adhesive as he reached under his shirt and yanked something free. "Aunt, get Kadee on." He cupped the device in his hand, hiding it from view. I caught a glimpse of fabric tape hanging from his palm. Definitely a spy. He'd probably been recording every conversation he had since arriving in NORA.

"Hold on," Rosa's voice said.

There was fumbling on the other end for a full minute, then the sound of light breathing. "What?" a woman's voice snapped. "This isn't what I gave it to you for, Chadd"

"Ma'am, I have Legacy Hawking here." Chadd's cross expression was gone now, replaced with a very real fear. "She demands to speak with you."

Kadee grunted. "Well, now you've compromised our communications, so this had better be good."

Chadd looked at me, hesitated, and placed a tiny black square box into my hand. His eyes gripped it as if he worried I'd take off running with it. I examined it and nearly laughed. This technology had to be at least four decades old. Was that one reason Kadee dealt with Virgil—because they needed better technology?

"Speak, Legacy Hawking," Kadee said impatiently.

Kole kept his stunner on Chadd, giving me an encouraging nod. It lent me the strength I needed, and I reminded myself I was a Hawking. In a second, I felt presence fall upon my shoulders once again.

"I'm here to renegotiate," I said evenly.

"Now?" Kadee chuckled darkly. "I gave you the chance. You scorned the idea, remember?"

"You lied about your bargain with Virgil, so I'm considering this an extension of our original negotiations. Tell me what you both agreed."

"First, tell me what you've observed," she said. "What do you think will happen to NORA next?"

I gritted my teeth. I should have known she'd try to play her games. "I know you've been collecting old NORA technology for Virgil, including anything associated with the Ratings and this odd little receiver here. You never intended to make a deal with me at all. Or am I wrong about that?"

"My bargain with him was a trade deal," she said quickly. "Nothing more. He gave us what we needed to take back the lands that are ours. We both know that would require taking the rest of NORA as well. Since your people would never accept an outsider to rule them, I had thought to put you on the throne under my direction. Virgil wouldn't have been happy about the arrangement, but it wasn't his decision to make."

"Why?" I demanded. "Why me and not my brother, or Virgil, or Chadd, for fates sake?"

She was quiet for a long moment. "Because you carry a part of us in your blood. You could have been a bridge to peace. I thought we both wanted that."

"We do. *I* do," I said. "But conquering NORA and putting me on the throne isn't peace."

"And how do you propose we put you on the throne, girl? By *not* conquering it? You think we can walk you up that sidewalk and into the building and place you in charge and all will be fine? That isn't how takeovers work. There is nothing clean about war, and that's exactly what this is. Your brother holds all the cards. It's far easier to work with him and your Virgil than it would have been with you. I chose to give you a chance anyway, yet you scorned it." I detected a hint of pain in her voice. She pretended not to care, but she did. Even Kadee couldn't remove the mother-daughter bond completely.

"I'm here now," I said softly. "I want you to end your dealings with Virgil. Destroy the remaining materials for the Ratings and refuse to assist him in any way. Send me troops to serve under my command. When I've taken the Copper Office and the military back, your soldiers will return home in peace."

"Like before, I fail to see what we get out of this, Legacy Hawking."

I glanced at Kole. He watched me with little expression, his eyes wary and full of gravity yet trusting. Whatever I chose to do, he would support me.

I lifted the box to my mouth. "Help me take the throne, and I promise you here and now that I will restore every centimeter of your former lands to you and your people. We'll live together as neighbors, just like you wanted."

The line was quiet.

"Legacy," Kole whispered, squinting. He hefted his stunner and aimed it into the darkness. "We aren't alone. It's time to go."

"I am willing to reconsider," Kadee finally said. "How do I know you will keep your end of the bargain?"

I blinked. I hadn't expected her to agree so quickly. Maybe our bond of blood meant more than I thought.

"We each have a witness here," I said, eyeing Chadd. He dipped his head once in acknowledgment. "Once I have the Copper Office back, we'll put it in writing. We'll even make an announcement." I imagined how that would go and felt my cheeks warm. I'd worry about it later. "There's one last thing. You know what it is." *The medicine.*

"You'll have it when this is all over and no sooner."

I looked at Kole, who seemed confused, and swallowed.

"Fine. I need four hundred soldiers at the station tomorrow night. They'll receive instructions then."

"There is just one complication," Kadee said. "We don't have sufficient weapons to arm four hundred soldiers. If you provide stunners, I will agree to your bargain."

Arming her soldiers with our weapons would not only give them power but effectively disarm us at the same time. I hesitated, feeling Kole's eyes on my face, irritated I knew so little about my own birth mother. Could she be trusted or not? She *had* allowed me to leave her underground city when I wanted, and Chadd had given me the space I needed since we arrived home.

"Well?" Kadee prodded.

There were so many ways this could go bad, but the alternative was certain to be worse. I needed an army in order to take the Block from my brother, and I refused to ask my supporters to become that army, not when they were untrained, unskilled, and in need of medical help. That left only one option—Kadee's army. My people would come to understand in time.

Kole placed his arm across my body protectively. "I think I saw some Firebrands on patrol," he hissed. "Time to wrap this up. We need to get back to the transport *now*."

"Kadee," I said into the receiver. "You have a deal."

TWENTY-SIX

KOLE

WE HID around the building until the patrol passed. The grounds were still quiet a few minutes later, so we crept toward the transport with our weapons raised. Travers hadn't left, which was either a good sign or a really bad one.

A few yards from the transport, I pulled Legacy to a halt and listened. The night was as quiet as before, but it felt too still, as if the very air were trying too hard to go unnoticed. The transport's windows were completely black. If Travers still sat inside, I couldn't see him. I lifted the stunner, motioned for Legacy to stay back in the shadows, and crept forward.

A dozen figures sprang from behind the transport and surrounded me in seconds, leveling their stunners at me. I went still, inwardly pleading for Legacy to pull deeper into the darkness. The last strolled out with a casual air and motioned for me to hand him my weapon. "You aren't going to need that anymore."

Zenn.

I cursed inwardly. Of all times for him to take his revenge. They'd probably taken out Travers while we conversed with Kadee, oblivious. I lifted my arms, clutching my weapon between two fingers to look less threatening. Their eyes followed the stunner. Then I turned my head and called over my shoulder. "Legs, run!"

I expected to see a figure darting across the shadows. Instead, a whoosh of air came from her direction and smacked into the Firebrand closest to me. He hit the ground and moaned. A second collapsed without a sound. I hid a grin.

The weapons aimed at me swung toward the shadows, looking for the source.

Now.

I ducked and spun around, taking out another two with my stunner as they searched the darkness for Legacy. I rolled over the hood and dropped to the ground just as a shot struck the transport, making the metal reverberate with a low hum. My hurt ribs screamed in protest. Someone shouted, then a furious exchange of wind and sound echoed across the parking lot. I ducked around the front and shot at a pair of legs that immediately collapsed, giving me a perfect shot at the guy's back.

I took down two more Firebrands, a man and a woman, before a couple of the others came around the transport for me. I quickly looked inside—no Travers—and scrambled around to the other side, shocked to find so many unconscious Firebrands on the ground. I didn't know Legacy was that good of a shot.

The transport's metal shell rang again, and the figures following me stiffened and collapsed. Only one left now. If I could just get to the shadows where Legacy waited . . .

A cold barrel pressed against my temple. "Drop the stunner, Kole," Zenn said.

I straightened, lifting my arms to the dark night sky. My

gut wrenched as three figures emerged from the darkness—two Firebrands and Legacy, her arms secured behind her back. She made them drag her by the elbows, digging her feet into the ground with each step. They weren't alone. Two more Firebrands dragged Travers just behind her. It was hard to see in the shadows of a distant streetlamp, but his face looked a little discolored. He hadn't given up without a fight.

"Drop it now," Zenn snapped.

I tossed my stunner aside. A second later, someone grabbed my arms from behind and snapped them into cuffs. They shoved Legacy and Travers to my side, making Legacy stumble.

"Watch it," I growled.

"I kinda hoped you'd fight harder," Zenn said. "Give us an excuse to shoot you. Dane wanted us to bring you in for him to deal with, but weapons malfunction all the time. Right, guys?"

The others laughed.

"He'll be happy with these two, though." He grinned at Legacy, who glowered back. "Kole and I have a reckoning of sorts."

Legacy shot a worried glance in my direction.

"Not in front of them," I snapped, my heart pounding so loudly I could almost hear it. "This is between you and me."

"What, you don't want your girlfriend to see us beat the living fates out of you?"

I wasn't surprised. It was exactly what I would have done in his place just months before. But Legacy had changed me. *Life* had changed me. "No, because we have something to discuss."

Now the Firebrands roared with laughter. Zenn stared

at me with narrowed eyes. "You can't talk your way out of this one, Kole. I had jaw surgery because of you. It even came out of my pay."

Legacy and Travers looked at each other in confusion. Good. Neither one knew about the day I'd lost my wits. Better that it die with me.

"Put them in the transport," I said. "You can bring us all in after you've taken your revenge. But first, we need to have a chat. Bring some of your buddies if you want."

Zenn's grip on his stunner only tightened. "What are you playing at, Kole? I don't need your permission to take what's mine."

"No, you don't," I agreed, feeling oddly at peace with what was about to happen. Whether my plan worked or not, at least my conscience would be clear at last. "And you owe me nothing. But I'm asking anyway. Let's do this in private."

He looked back and forth between the others, then growled. "Fine. Put the others in the transport. Make sure they're secure and keep three stunners on them at all times. The rest of you, see to the fallen."

"You want help, Zenn?" Lorna, one of Dane's recruits from last year, practically purred the question. Interesting. That had to be new.

He shoved his weapon into fatal mode with a decisive click. Several others in the group flinched. "No, I'm good. Never been better."

Lorna shrugged and bent over a body on the ground.

Legacy fought against being shoved into the transport, but Zenn didn't let me stand around and watch for long. He pushed me toward the very shadows that had hidden Legacy a minute before. When we were out of earshot, he whirled me around and placed his stunner against my head again.

That weird peace settled even deeper, calming the flips in my stomach.

"You can start begging now. I won't judge." He smirked. "*Too* much."

I thought of Legacy in that transport and Dane waiting for her. That hardened my resolve immediately. "I didn't bring you here to beg. You deserve justice after what I did, you and the others too. No, I wanted to tell you why I'm not like my father. First, I'm about to apologize to you."

His eyes widened. "The great Kole Mason, nephew of Dane Mason, says he's sorry? That's a first."

"I forgot who my enemies were and took my anger at Dane out on you. That wasn't fair. I don't agree with what Dane's doing, but that doesn't justify turning against my friends like some robotic assassin. I'm horrified I acted that way. Second, I'm going to ask you for something I don't deserve. I need your forgiveness."

My former friend looked taken aback for a moment, then chuckled. "Yeah. You almost had me there for a second."

"Zenn, I'm not like my father because . . . because I killed him to save my Mom's life." There. I'd said it.

Zenn took a step back, surprise registering on his face, but he kept the stunner trained on me. "And that's supposed to make me trust you?"

"I had to choose between an abusive father and an innocent mother. One of them was going to die that night. So I chose the one who made the world better." I saw figures approach in the shadows and raised my voice so they could hear. "It's the same choice all of us have to make. Not next week or next year, but right now. One side is going to win, so which will it be? Virgil and his Rating system and manipulations, or Legacy and a fresh start with a slew of changes? Which will make the world better? I think you already know the answer to that, or you would have killed me by now."

Zenn's face darkened again. "You deserted us, remember? We swore to band together, to defend and protect one another. It was always us against them, and you joined them."

I shook my head. "No. That's what Dane says, but it's wrong. It was never us against them, Zenn. Life is more complicated than that. Firebrand oath or not, what Dane's doing is wrong, and you know it."

"I don't know what you're talking about."

"Pretty sure you do. All those patients you denied hospital treatment to, the families with sick parents you turned away, the stores you ransacked for supplies that had to close against hungry neighborhoods, the homeless you implanted under Dane's orders. There are kids who can't sleep at night knowing the Firebrands roam the streets, afraid you'll light them up in their beds. If we have to become the bad guys to accomplish what we want, maybe what we want was wrong in the first place."

He hesitated. "Or maybe it's like they say. The end justifies the means."

"Do you like this end? You can see now where Dane is taking us. Do you agree with his vision for NORA?"

He looked stricken. "The Rating system is what we've worked for all this time."

"No, *equality* is what we've worked for all this time. Freedom for everyone, no matter where they were born or what they look like or how many credits they have in their account. The Rating system's version of equality is synthetic. If we have to rely on the government to make everyone equal, it means we've failed to do it ourselves. That's on us. *All of us.* Believe me, I get what it's like to get beat up and have my things stolen and be so hungry my stomach feels like it's caving in. I know what people think when they look at you because I see it in their eyes when they look at me too. Violence can change borders and leaders and even laws, but it doesn't change minds, and it certainly doesn't change hearts." I looked him right in the eyes. "So I'm asking you again to forgive me even though I don't deserve it. I need another chance to do what Dane won't. I want to help save this country—me and Legacy and whoever else wants to do this the right way."

My friend's hand shook on the stunner. He stared down the barrel, his eyes intense and hard. I stood still, waiting, not daring to move a single tendon should his finger slip on the trigger. It felt like an eternity before he lowered his weapon.

"I trusted you," he snapped. "Worshipped you, maybe. You were everything, and when you left, we all felt lost."

I nodded. "I should have explained and given you the chance to join me. That was stupid."

"Yep," Lorna said, stepping out of the shadows. "Definitely stupid, and attacking three Firebrands at HQ? Tragic, I'm telling you. But I never liked that guy you shot anyway. Couldn't keep his hands to himself. I guess it wouldn't be so bad to show Dane what's what." She turned to Zenn with a smirk. "Came for another reason, though. After Legacy Hawking told us about Kole's little condition, I came to make sure he didn't play the 'I'm dying so you owe me' card."

Zenn cocked an eyebrow at me.

I tried to look unaffected, but inside my stomach

crawled. My condition? What did Legacy know that I didn't? I forced a smile and said the first thing that came to mind. "I don't plan to die anytime soon."

A short, squat guy materialized next to the girl. "I'm with Lorna and Kole. I don't like what we're doing either."

Squinting, I could barely make out the outlines of half a dozen of Firebrands in the shadows. They'd been listening all along. They held their stunners at their sides too.

"My apology extends to all of you," I said. "Whether you choose to join us or not."

They murmured agreement with various degrees of enthusiasm. Inside, I felt a little thrill.

I turned to Zenn. "How about it?"

He looked around and rubbed the dark stubble on his jaw with his free hand. "I'm in, but there's one thing I'm not willing to give up quite yet."

"What's tha—"

The punch came before I was ready, and it threw me sideways. I stumbled and worked my jaw to make sure it still functioned. "I deserved that."

"Yes, you did." Zenn was smiling.

———

ONLY ONE FIREBRAND remained as we reached the transport again. Zenn stunned the guy, insisting he was nearly as bad as Dane, then dragged him out of the seat and put him next to the pile of other unconscious Firebrands. Legacy looked on with wide eyes from the back seat. As they freed her and Travers from their bonds, I slid into the seat next to her.

She stared at me in wonder. "Maybe you should have Declared to be a city defender."

"Defenders have to lie all the time. Every word I said was true." I looked at her, trying to decipher the secrets she carried in that beautiful head of hers.

"What?" she asked.

"Did you tell them I'm dying?"

I'd hoped she would laugh and say she made it up, but she swallowed and shifted in her seat. Then I knew.

The damage from Virgil's experiment. The nightmares, the attacks. They were all related. That had to be what Legacy had danced around in her conversation with Kadee.

Another headache lurked behind my eyes. The world pulled in a bit, slightly blurring around the edges.

"I know how to help you," Legacy said. "We just have to win this first. I promise it will all work out." She didn't sound convinced.

Zenn climbed into the front. "So, what now?" He looked incredulous, as if still unable to believe what he'd just agreed to do.

"Head for the Shadows," Legacy told him. "We have a safe house there, an abandoned gym that we aren't using anymore. We can discuss the plan there." Her voice had a hollow ring to it.

Zenn gave the transport directions and settled back, batting away the harness that swung down from the top. Lorna dove in and sat next to him, whispering into his ear. He grinned wickedly as the transport pulled away. The second transport immediately fell in line behind us, carrying the five other recruits. Smart of Legacy to use the empty safe house, just in case anyone changed their mind. We'd drop them off and continue to the island on our own. Then we'd return tomorrow night with every weapon we could find and a contingent of soldiers ready for action. The thought felt distant, like a city skyline across a channel.

I had no idea whether the specialist was right about my destiny. But then, I didn't know a lot of things, like how Legacy and I would combine our very different lives into a lasting relationship. I didn't know where I would live or what job to take when this all ended. All I knew was that we were *so* close to seeing this through, and I wanted to be there for all of it. I wanted to watch Legacy grow into her role in the Copper Office. I had to show her I trusted her and I wasn't going anywhere, no matter what nightmares took hold of me or what impulsive rampages I had to fight off.

I'd never cared what anyone else thought about my capabilities before. I wasn't about to start now.

Legacy scooted closer and placed her head on my shoulder. I reached down and took her hand, threading our fingers together.

We didn't say a word the entire ride back.

TWENTY-SEVEN

LEGACY

T<small>HEN NEXT DAY PASSED QUICKLY</small>, partly because of the preparations that needed to be made and partly because Kole and I took turns sleeping, resting up for Kadee's soldiers to arrive that night. I recruited Foster to do the hardest part of all—gather as many stunners as he could and transport them to the safe house, no questions asked. He seemed to know our intentions because he also arrived with a small contingent of guards. They'd insisted on coming, he said, but I knew the truth. It had Gram's orders written all over it.

As promised, four hundred soldiers arrived in the dead of night. Chadd had cleared the station of security much like that first night I'd traveled with him, but even more remarkable was the fact that Dane's Firebrands didn't show up to stop us. It wasn't until we'd reached an old gym to hide the soldiers that Kole explained Zenn's hand in all of this. He'd paid a rival Shadow gang to stir up trouble at headquarters. By the time Dane realized something was happening at the Block, it would be too late to stop us.

We waited for hours in that gym, enduring heat and

body odor and several coughing soldiers who looked like they hadn't seen a shower in weeks. It felt like at least three nights before Foster peeked his head in and said it was nearly five.

An hour later, the moment arrived.

I flattened myself against the brick wall of a building across the street from the Block, brushing the shoulder of the soldier next to me. His felt as bony as Chadd looked. My supporters looked positively huge next to most of Kadee's fighters, who sported narrower frames and gaunt cheeks, their dark-green uniforms looking to be a century old. The soldiers didn't talk much either, watching suspiciously, as if the city would crumble down on their heads.

As the sun climbed and cast long shadows across the road, I tried to see all this from their point of view. A city this size would certainly have seemed a marvel after a lifetime underground or living in the ruins of destroyed border towns. That, if nothing else, seemed a good reason for my bargain with Kadee. I clung to that thought as the sick feeling in my stomach grew.

This was the right thing to do. Our deal meant help for her people and freedom for mine. We would prevent the world's leaders from getting technology that could hurt an unfathomable number of people. I would get medicine for Kole and buy Millian time to heal many of our patients, including Dad. Kadee's soldiers would be gone before most of NORA even knew what had happened. Anyone in my position would have been patting themselves on the back. It was the perfect plan.

So why did I feel like this was the biggest mistake I'd ever made?

I resisted the urge to peek around the corner at the Block. Reports said Alex hadn't left last night, which meant he'd taken to sleeping in the Copper Office. It also meant more guards to incapacitate on our way in. Thankfully, we'd chosen early morning for our raid since most of the city would still be safe in their homes. The Malrain soldiers, led by our new Firebrand recruits and a few select followers with Enforcer training, had orders not to hurt any civilians. I'd armed them with nearly every weapon we owned, giving strict orders to use stun mode only. I'd thought of everything. Hadn't I?

Kole, wearing a protective helmet and serving as a captain over twenty Malrain soldiers, caught my eye across the street. He crouched behind a building much like ours, his twenty soldiers circling him and listening while he gave directions. I smiled at seeing him in his element before remembering what was at stake. I'd tried to convince him to go to the island in case he got triggered again, but the more evidence I presented, the more stubborn he grew.

"Not a chance," he'd said. "We had a deal. We stay together."

A solitary transport drifted past, followed by a long silence. No more traffic. Travers had succeeded in getting the construction barricades up on either end of the street. The time was almost here.

"Ten minutes," whispered the figure crouched next to me. His whisper sounded in my earpiece a hair's breadth after it left his lips, and I knew the other troops hidden around the Block had heard. Kadee would be listening to this feed as well, I knew. She had more to lose today than I did.

I patted my stunner, surprised at the comfort I took from it lately. I barely felt it at my hip these days.

Soon, our mission leader, a former Enforcer who had joined my supporters near the beginning, barked her orders.

"Team one, advance." Then a long pause. "Team two, advance."

Kole sent me a sharp look as if warning me back, then rose and trotted down the street. He needn't have worried. My team wouldn't allow me to fight if I'd ordered them to. No, my stunner would be used for another purpose.

Five more teams joined them over the next two minutes. I listened hard, barely daring to breathe, before I finally heard it. A shout from the Block.

The fighting had begun.

My earpiece filled with the sounds of shouting and grunts and orders. When the mission leader didn't call for more troops, hope swelled inside. Maybe it was going better than planned and they wouldn't need the rest. Maybe nobody would get hurt or die today after all. Relief joined my hope as I looked at the troops waiting for their turn. Since our weapons had run out, these soldiers held guns with real bullets. Once they began using those, the entire city would know we were here.

And soon the entire city and my cabinet would know I was a traitor too. Eventually, the council members would discover I'd only sent them away to keep them safe.

The horrible sounds in my earpiece went quiet.

Soldiers reporting to their commanders in low tones filled my ears now, their words blending in a quiet cacophony of nonsense.

The soldier next to me relaxed and grinned.

I looked at him quizzically, then at the others. "Is that it? Did we win? Where is Alex?"

Our captain, the Firebrand recruit named Rosa, looked at me with annoyance. "We have him, but he called for reinforcements before his capture. Now the battle truly begins." She lifted her stunner. "I hope this is what you wanted, *Your Honor*, because it's too late to go back now."

I clamped my mouth and tried to wait, but my nerves felt jumpy and skittish. I wanted to be inside with Kole and those soldiers, to explain to my brother that everything would be okay—and if he tried to fight, I would stun him myself. I wanted to sit at that desk and make an announcement to the country that this was all over and we could begin the healing process at last. I wanted to be able to tell Dad when he woke that we'd done it and the country was ours once again.

Instead, I leaned against a rough brick building with a sick heart, dying for the news that would change our lives.

"They're ready for us," Rosa said. "Team, you will protect Her Honor at all costs. March!"

My stomach leaped ahead of my feet, and soon we were trotting down the street after her, carrying our weapons in both hands, scouring the street for any sign of danger as we approached the Block. A crowd swarmed the front lawn. Occasionally, I caught a glimpse of an anxious face in a building window. I had no doubt these stores had locked their occupants in.

It made me feel like an invader more than a leader, and I didn't like it.

As we arrived, the Malrain soldiers lined up in formation outside the building, leaving a straight path to the front doors. I wanted to stride in like I had a hundred times, to set foot in Dad's office and see him smiling at his desk. But no, it was Alex I had come to see and Dad's office I had come to seize.

Today I wasn't a daughter but an invader.

It seemed an eternity before Kole and Zenn emerged from the building, shoving Alex out in front of them. I exhaled, feeling the tension in my shoulders relax slightly. Everyone looked fine. Maybe this would go as planned after all.

Alex glowered at me as they pushed him toward me. "Malrain soldiers, huh, *sister*? That's low, even for you."

"Oh, so I can't work with them, but you and Virgil can? That makes total sense."

He blinked, looking genuinely confused. "I didn't— wait, why did you think that? I allowed Virgil to lease some equipment and buy supplies for his lab. That's it."

So Virgil had made arrangements on his own. That didn't surprise me. "Virgil always meant to overthrow you, Alex. You're lucky we beat him to it. Now we can stop him together."

Alex's jaw clenched as he took in the army standing behind me. The glint in his eyes was all fight and no acceptance. "Looks to me like you joined our enemies, Legacy, not the other way around. Whatever they told you, they lied, like always. If you'd ever come to the office with me, you'd know Dad's been trying to sign a treaty with them for years. Every time Malrain agrees to something, they break their word within weeks. They can't be trusted to fulfill a trade agreement, let alone a military alliance." He shook his head. "I bet you don't even know about the train, do you?"

A chill crept over me despite the heat. "What about it?"

"We intercepted a train full of Malrain soldiers about an hour ago. Since my Firebrands were occupied elsewhere, they easily took the station and everything else within two blocks of it. They have hostages and everything. I'm willing to bet there will be more on the way. I was dealing with that when your boyfriend dragged me from my chair." He glared at Kole, who grunted.

That familiar strangling sensation returned. I heard my breaths coming in a series of ragged gasps.

A train full of soldiers.

I'd half expected Kadee to order her soldiers to turn on us, and I'd prepared my troops for that possibility. But I'd never considered that Kadee would send additional soldiers on a different mission. No wonder she'd given in to our negotiations so quickly. Clearly she meant to take over the city on her terms while we were distracted here. Once we took the Copper Office, it would be nothing to unseat me. She'd get everything she wanted with barely any cost to herself.

Kole pulled his helmet off and dropped it to the ground, staring at me with dread. He'd just realized the same thing.

In trying to save my country, I'd doomed it.

A siren sounded several blocks away, then another, closer.

"They're getting closer," Alex said. "You'd better—"

The soldier to my right cocked his weapon and placed it at my temple. It felt cold against my skin. A metal barrel. I went still, barely daring to breathe. This was no stunner.

He tore my weapon from my hands and straightened, his gaze sweeping the crowd of green before us as the other soldiers swung their weapons at my supporters. At least ten kept theirs on Alex. I counted four guns aimed at his head.

"Every NORA soldier will put their weapons down now," my captor said.

Kole's eyes widened as he lifted his arms to the sky, his stunner hanging loosely in his hand like it had two days ago. Except this time, there would be no sweet-talking our way out of this. Even Zenn set his stunner down and raised his hands, eyeing me warily.

"Alex," I called to my brother, "I'm sorry, but I'll make this right."

My brother gave a dark chuckle. "You opened the gates, sister. It's too late to close them now."

"Unit Blue, come with me," my captor shouted. "Bring the brother too. There's someone waiting for them in the Copper Office."

I held Kole's gaze as the soldiers shoved me toward the doors, watching his dismay turn into a terrible pain that hurt my chest. Then the darkness of the Block swallowed me up.

TWENTY-EIGHT

LEGACY

VIRGIL SAT at my father's desk, hunched over the glass screen. "Well, well. Look at all these breaches. Never thought I'd see the day a Hawking allowed Malrain to conquer us." He glanced up at me. "Or maybe not such a Hawking after all?" The burns I'd given him at Neuromen gave his face sinister shadows that seemed very appropriate.

"Get out of my father's chair," I growled.

"So possessive. Speaking of your father, I want you to tell me where he is."

Alex slowly lifted his head to meet my gaze. I'd spent the past weeks sure that the brother I knew was dead, replaced by a stranger who wanted Dad to die. He'd nearly told me as much in our last conversation. But I saw a different truth in his eyes now, one that reminded me of the brother I thought I'd lost.

Don't tell him, he seemed to say. *Keep Dad safe.*

I raised my chin, feeling the gun against my temple tighten. "You're going to kill us anyway, so why would I tell you anything?"

"Because despite the way you spoiled children have

acted over the past weeks, you care about each other. I'll wager that neither of you wants to watch the other die. The question is, which sibling to choose?"

"How dare you," Alex growled with gritted teeth. "You said I could trust you."

"I said you could trust me to help secure the country, and I kept that promise. You only assumed I meant under your hand. You didn't really think we meant to keep you in power long, did you? The nation has spoken. The Hawking dynasty ends today."

"This isn't how you end a line of succession," I snapped. "You don't get to march in here and kill the entire family. The people will never accept you if you try."

"They'll never know. We've been conquered by Malrain soldiers, after all. Haven't you heard? They can be brutal in their methods. Assassinating an entire family is exactly what everyone would expect from them."

The soldier standing next to me stiffened, but his weapon didn't lower.

Virgil turned off the desk screen and rose to his feet. "But assassination is the messier of our two options here. Once your sister has revealed the location of your comatose father, young Alexandrite, I will allow you to make one last public announcement. You will tell your supporters you've decided to turn the reins over to someone with more leadership experience. The transition will be both pain-free and bloodless."

"You always wanted the throne," Alex said, his voice trembling with anger. "This was your plan all along."

I shot my brother a look of pity. I wasn't the only one who'd trusted the wrong people. Now we'd both suffer for it.

Virgil threw back his balding head and laughed. "Ah,

but my sights have been set quite a bit higher for some time now. You children have never crossed our borders. You don't know the world beyond, much less the potential it holds."

"I've been to Malrain, and I like NORA much better," I snapped. "As it is now, though—not controlled by a Rating system that turns people into mindless robots."

"The people disagree with you, then, young Legacy, because the response to our announcement has been over-whelmingly positive. Your citizens are ready for a change, Hawkings. They're willing to give up a little freedom to live a better life."

"They shouldn't have to give up *any* freedom," I said quietly.

Virgil stepped around the desk and stopped in front of me. "It's a trade most of us make every day—spend your day lining someone else's pockets and live in a warm home with food to eat, or sleep on the streets in total freedom and starve. You aren't immune to such choices either. Your grandmother and father traded their family for power. Alex betrayed his father to take that power. You betrayed the country to take it from him. If we allow this to continue, we'll have more of the same." He stepped up to me, standing so close I caught a whiff of antiseptic that brought me back to my days at Neuromen. "Your people are tired, Legacy Hawking. Can you blame them?"

I lowered my head. Virgil had done terrible things, but about this one thing, I had to admit he was right.

Virgil frowned. "Now, tell me where your father is, and we can end this peacefully." He leaped toward Alex and swept the gun from his guard in one swift movement. A second later, it was Virgil who held a gun to my brother's head. A real gun. "Right now."

A strangled gasp came from Alex's throat, and his eyes flew open, but he went still and tense.

"That won't be necessary, Director." A figure entered the room. This time, I was too shocked to do anything but gape.

Dad.

The air around us seemed to change. The Malrain soldiers seemed to shrink, and the room somehow grew bigger, brighter. Everything was as it should be. The Copper Office's true owner had finally arrived. Dad would know what to do. He would fix this.

Then I saw the guards on either side of him and his arms locked behind his back, and reality struck me with its cruel truth yet again.

As the shock wore off and the joy at seeing him on his feet—so normal, so usual, yet so *incredible*—dissipated, I took note of the little details that meant all wasn't well. The dark skin under his eyes. His slightly hunched shoulders. The way he dragged his feet as if barely able to move them. How his hands trembled, barely visible beneath his shirt cuffs. He'd put on regular clothes, but they clearly weren't his. The sleeves hung too long, the waist was too baggy, the trousers too short.

Regardless, Virgil looked ready to fall over. "How?" he managed. "When?"

Dad's eyes stopped on the gun at my head. "Our laboratory head discovered Legacy's plan and made a quick decision. Before you try to damage my mind even further, I assure you I've been freed from the clutches of your brain implant for nearly twenty-four hours now. My healing will continue long after we're done here." He walked over and claimed a space between me and Alex, forcing his guards to scramble to keep their weapons trained on him. "Now, remove those weapons from my children so we can begin our negotiations."

Virgil leaned against the desk as if to remind himself that it belonged to him now. "I don't negotiate."

"Oh?" Kadee said from the doorway. "You seem to enjoy it quite a bit, if I recall."

TWENTY-NINE

LEGACY

Dad groaned, and Virgil's expression darkened.

The Malrain leader barely sent me a glance as she headed toward the desk and sat down in the chair. "You're a smart man, Virgil. Surely you remember the terms of our agreement. I take NORA and everything the Hawkings have built for myself. You rebuild Neuromen and head your Ratings project. Everybody leaves happy."

Virgil glared at her so fiercely I expected him to lunge at any second. But he folded his arms instead. "Of course. That was always the plan."

I may have been a terrible liar, but I knew one when I saw one. Virgil intended to keep exactly none of his promises to Kadee, just as she'd dodged her promises to me. They deserved each other.

She turned to Dad. "How nice to see you again, Honorable Malachite Hawking. This is far more pleasant than the last time we met in person. Do you remember the rain?"

Dad's eyes lowered.

My stomach sank as I looked at each of them in turn. "What happened last time?"

"I discovered the criminal who'd stolen my child and visited his home, desperate to see her again. You would have been about three, Legacy. It poured rain that night, and the water filled my boots to the brim. When I knocked on the door, soaked to the skin, your father assumed I'd come to kidnap you and shot me. I awoke, dumped at the border, surrounded by NORA soldiers and still drenched in rain with a massive bruise on my face."

I turned to Dad, expecting him to deny it, but he fell silent. A mixture of horror and sorrow churned inside me.

"I returned a few nights later with my own weapon. This time guards greeted me at the door and took it, but I saw him hiding behind them. I offered him a deal. If he returned my daughter, he could keep everything else he owned. If not . . ."

"You would take it," I whispered.

"Everything," Kadee confirmed with a nod.

I stared at Dad. "You told me there was nobody by that name. You lied to me."

"Yes, and I shouldn't have. I wanted to protect you."

I wanted to protect you. His excuse sounded much like mine when I hid my nighttime mission from Kole. I'd felt so justified. The hurt I felt now—was this a portion of how he'd felt then?

"You didn't want to give me the choice," I said, not hiding the accusation in my voice. "In case I chose her *and* a normal life. It would have ruined the entire family."

His eyes looked sad. "It was a mistake, perhaps the greatest I've ever committed. I'm sorry, both of you."

Kadee chuckled. "Well, now I have my daughter back, Hawking, and she's delivered your country to me. It's time to keep my promise." She swung the weapon and aimed it at my father.

I yelped and struggled to free myself to prevent the execution, but Dad just stood there, looking down the long barrel with a calculating eye.

"You're wrong, Kadee Steer," he said calmly.

"I'm never wrong," the woman snapped.

"You said my daughter handed you my country. She may think so, but she didn't. Legacy didn't have authorization to make such a bargain, and neither did Alex. Had I been in charge, I couldn't have done so either. An international alliance requires the signatures of at least two-thirds of the War and Trade Councils. It says so in the NORA Decision Declaration." His gaze locked on me. "A protection drafted by my mother, the Honorable Treena Hawking, to ensure no individual holds too much power."

I gave him a tiny smile, which he returned.

Kadee lifted her head from the gun. "I don't see how any of this is relevant. We've taken NORA, and your citizens will soon fall in line. I can draft whatever new measures I want."

"Again, you're wrong," Dad said. "Our country is more than the government building you've taken, and terrorizing a few public places will earn you nothing but fear. You can sit in the Copper Office. You can use Virgil's tech to hurt people or threaten their loved ones. You can even end the Hawking line, here and now. But that doesn't make you NORA's leader. It makes you their enemy, and they won't stand for it for long. We're accustomed to freedom here. There will be no going back. It goes deeper than our politics—it's in our blood." He looked directly into her eyes. "However, I know how much you love negotiations. Release Legacy and Alex unharmed, and I will sign the Honorship over to you."

"Dad, no," I moaned.

"You said such a thing couldn't be done without a committee," Kadee said.

"I can't give you my country, but I can give you my position. You'll be able to appoint your own followers to the council then. That is my offer."

A glint of triumph entered Kadee's eyes, and she lowered the weapon. "And you'll make an announcement to your people, telling them of our agreement, to smooth the transition?"

Something thumped down the hall.

Kadee jerked her attention away from Dad, looking around the room. "Where is Virgil?"

I'd been so occupied with Kadee and Dad's conversation, I hadn't seen him leave. Now I heard a popping sound coming from outside.

Kadee pointed at the soldiers guarding us. "You and you. See what's going on and report. Make sure the doors are secured."

The guard at my side rushed off, followed by Alex's. Only Dad's two guards remained. They looked at Alex and me as if unsure where to aim their weapons and finally kept them trained on Dad.

"They can't possibly be fighting back," Kadee muttered. "Not as outnumbered as they are."

Dad remained silent as Kadee paced the office, waiting for the guards to return and mumbling to herself. I shot him a curious look, but he shook his head slightly. Then I understood.

He'd been buying us time.

"What is taking them so long?" she snapped a minute later, stalking to the door. She hefted her gun and reached for the handle.

The door slammed open, and Kole sprinted inside, sending Kadee stumbling backward.

Everything happened in slow motion. The soldiers guarding Dad leaped to her aid, brushing past me, and I watched as Kole lifted a stunner and took aim. It connected with the guard closest to him, sending the man to the floor. But the one just in front of me trained his pistol on Kole.

"No!" I shouted and charged, throwing myself into his shoulder.

The weapon jumped sideways just as he pulled the trigger.

The sound slammed into my eardrums, but I ignored the pain as I stumbled to my feet, barely noticing the scent of gunpowder in the air. Kole stood straight and tall and healthy, staring at Kadee in horror.

My biological mother placed a hand to her chest and pulled it away.

It was then I saw the blood seeping through her shirt.

Kole threw out his arms just in time. She collapsed, and he half caught her, half eased her to the ground.

Everyone in the room went still. The shooter's eyes widened as he realized what he'd done. His weapon hung in one hand, his shoulders limp as Kole stood. Both looked down at Kadee. She lay on her back now, her hair splayed out around her, staring at the copper ceiling with eyes that looked like mine. Eyes that had already begun to fade.

Her shooter swore, dropped his weapon with a clang, and bolted. Kole stepped aside to allow his escape.

I went to her, the woman who'd given me life, if nothing else, and knelt at her side. My knees grew wet with warm blood. Her eyes found mine, and she tried to say something, but blood filled the spaces between her teeth, and the only sound that emerged was a strained gurgle from her throat.

"I know," I told her gently, seeing the silent wish on her face. "I would have liked that too."

It was the right thing to say. She relaxed, then released a gentle, quiet breath, letting her eyes close.

Silence.

I leaned over and placed my fingers on the side of her throat. No pulse. Kadee Steer had made it to the Copper Office, but she would make it no further.

I brushed her hair out of her face. Its texture felt much like mine. If things had been different, would we have brushed one another's hair and shared gossip? Would it have been Kadee who sat on my bed at night, listening to my petty worries and offering advice? Would she have been driven to climb the ranks of Malrain and take her revenge on NORA?

Kole leaned down and pulled me into his arms. "I'm sorry. I know you had a complicated relationship. What did you tell her you would have liked?"

I looked down at the woman who'd given me life. "A choice," I admitted. "In the end, I wouldn't have chosen the life she offered, but I would have welcomed starting over in the future."

We stood there for a long moment, me saying goodbye and Kole right where I needed him to be.

The other guard stood in front of Dad with unblinking eyes, staring at my blood-soaked knees in a state of shock, the color drained from his face.

"You'd better join the others," Dad told him gently. "They'll be retreating to the train station about now."

The guard tore his gaze away from Kadee, blinking at us like he'd forgotten we were there. He considered Dad's words, then let his shoulders slump. He stumbled toward the door, giving Kadee one last look, as if considering whether to bring her body, then sprinted out the door empty-handed.

"Why would they be retreating?" Alex asked.

Dad smiled. "I didn't come alone."

THIRTY

KOLE

LEGACY and I sat on a bench outside as workers cleared the grounds of the wounded and dead. Zenn stood guard nearby despite the fact that there wasn't a single Malrain soldier in sight. He winked as I stroked Legacy's arm, letting her sink into me as the tension she'd carried over the past few months slowly drained away.

It was over.

"I can't believe Millian did that," Legacy said, chuckling to herself. "Imagine it—Millian the scientist waving a stunner around a broadcasting station and demanding they put her on camera. They probably thought she was mad."

"Whatever they said, people liked it," I told her, remembering the moment Millian's army had arrived. It seemed like half the city had descended upon Kadee's army at once, sending the streets into a frenzy. I couldn't believe how many civilians had weapons. They'd probably inherited them from original NORA citizens.

"It proves Virgil was wrong," Legacy said. "They don't want the Rating system. They just want change, and that's something they deserve." She stared at her feet. "Especially after today."

I grabbed her hand. "They like that you've helped so many people. What surprised me was how many came over from the island. They were excited to finally make a difference."

Her tone was one of wonder. "I underestimated them because of their needs. I shouldn't have. Millian was right all along. I wasn't the only person with someone to lose."

"You made some mistakes, but somehow it turned out all right. Your dad has his throne back, Alex is a little more humble than he was yesterday, and the comatose patients have a good prognosis for the first time in weeks. I'd say this was a success."

Legacy turned away.

"What?" I asked, concerned. "I know what happened to Kadee has to be hard, but—"

"Your medicine," Legacy said softly. "Kadee discovered a cure for your condition. Or maybe she developed it—I don't really know. She promised to give it to me when this was all over. I can't exactly walk into Malrain and ask for it now."

I paused, gathering my thoughts. "We didn't think we could find a solution to your dad's issue, yet he's fine. We'll figure this out too. Besides, I've made it this long. I haven't even had a nightmare since before . . ." *That night.* She made a face, obviously hearing what I wasn't saying. "Maybe being unconscious served as a reset and I'm fine now."

"And the headaches?" she asked, looking up at me with doubt.

I was about to answer when the screaming began.

Leaping to my feet and pushing past the guards, I saw a mob in black uniforms making their way down the street toward us. I spotted weapons at their belts, but they didn't draw them. At their head was Dane.

He saw me, and our gazes locked.

Yes, something deep inside said. *Revenge at last.*

My uncle broke into a sinister smile and lengthened his stride, heading straight for me.

Zenn hurried to my side. "They didn't come here for the Copper Office. They know they'd lose. It's you he came for. The others will be here to make sure nobody interferes. If you run now, he won't catch you."

"Kole," Legacy snapped, shoving past Zenn. "You don't have to do this. If you get angry again—"

"I'm always angry. Maybe defeating my uncle will finally change that."

All I could see was my uncle's terrible smile, the one he always wore when pummeling me in a corner. It would give me great delight to return the favor.

This is it, Mom. I defended you once. Now, I avenge you.

"But, Kole—"

I whirled on her. "You wanted me to trust you, Legacy. You reminded me it was your decision and your life. At least allow me the same."

She looked stricken for a second, and I longed to pull her into my arms, but my uncle was almost here, and this wasn't something I wanted her to see.

"Zenn, get Legacy to safety," I said. "If Dane wins, he'll want the both of you."

My friend nodded and took Legacy's elbow. "Sorry, Your Honor, but he's right. Let's watch from a safer distance. Need to get a few more guards on you anyway."

As Zenn dragged Legacy toward the building, she turned her head to watch.

Then Dane arrived.

My uncle's hands were empty, but I spotted a distinct outline in both pockets. Even if I managed to steal one stunner, he had a second—and he undoubtedly had a knife hidden somewhere. Experience told me I wouldn't get close enough to reach any of them.

"I've waited for this a long while," Dane said.

I tried to keep my expression casual. "Really? I thought you were having too much fun burning children in their beds to notice I was gone."

"I'd burn down the entire city if it meant your demise, boy."

"Demise? You've expanded your vocabulary. Dad would have been pleased."

Dane's jaw clenched. Next came the purple in his face, and then he would snap. "You've no right to talk about my brother, much less carry his name. I should never have allowed you under my roof."

"Funny, because as I recall, I did everything you told me to do. I ran your errands, delivered your messages, and fulfilled your 'missions.' I even believed we would make a difference. Now, look at you. Look at *this*." I gestured to the square still being cleared of the injured and bodies covered with tarps and lined up neatly on the sidewalk. "Is this the future you planned for NORA? Did you really think I would cooperate while you murdered people? You couldn't honestly believe I'd watch you kill my mom and then slink away like nothing ever happened." Emotion choked the last few words, but I swallowed it back.

His eyes were hard. "Look at my nephew. So devastated to lose his mommy. I bet you cry at night."

I hadn't slept well a single night since Mom died, but Dane deserved no such satisfaction. When someone inflicted pain on him, he lashed out twice as hard to teach them a lesson. In that moment, I saw a chilling truth. As long as Dane lived, this would never be over. Now that he'd tasted victory, the Hawking family would never enjoy peace. The sadness of Mom's death receded like an ocean wave at high tide, quiet and inevitable in its strength. All that remained was the anger. Good. I preferred it that way.

"I don't cry at night," I told him. "I plan. You aren't the only one who has prepared for this moment. You'll feel every single pain you inflicted on my family before this day is done."

Dane's hand reached for the stunner to his right. I started to reach for mine before I remembered I'd given it to Legacy just an hour before. I grabbed a Firebrand who'd gotten too close by the collar, shoving him into Dane just as the stunner made an appearance. The two men stumbled as the stunner hit the ground. I ducked and swiped it, taking a quick look as they pushed apart. *Fatal mode.* Down the barrel was a long, sharp crack.

I cursed.

Sneering, Dane drew his other stunner. I threw the broken one at him, watched him dodge it, and then sprinted at one of the tarps near the sidewalk. I ducked instinctively as a rush of air whooshed by and then dove at the covered figures on the ground, feeling for weapons, trying not to think of the stench that wafted from underneath.

There. Something hard.

I rolled sideways to dodge another shot, then slid the weapon out. I rose to my feet, aimed, and squeezed the trigger.

The weapon bucked in my hand and caused a deaf-

ening roar. Those around me dropped to the ground—
everyone except Dane, who yelped and clutched at his
thigh. His other stunner lay on the ground as well.

I kicked it aside and intercepted his other arm just as
Dane leaped up, a knife flashing in his hand. We stood there
grunting, Dane trying to stab the blade into my heart, and
me struggling to keep him from doing just that. My
shoulder trembled from exertion and the exhaustion of the
morning. I watched as his wrist turned, trying to get a piece
of my arm instead, and I caught a glimpse of burned flesh
under his arm.

With a yell, I gathered my strength and shoved him
backward, following it up with a kick to his injured thigh.
Dane screamed and stumbled, but to his credit, he didn't
collapse.

"You set the fire, didn't you?" I shouted at him. "You
tried to kill me in my sleep, you coward."

He hunched over, trying to catch his breath. "I thought
of a hundred ways to do it, but they were all too quick. But
burning to death on the top floor of a building? They say fire
is the worst way to die."

I considered all the people who'd died in just that way—
the families and maybe even children, just because they
lived in the same building—and I pulled the trigger.

Nothing happened.

Frowning, I inspected the handle but couldn't figure out
how to reload the thing.

Dane smirked. "You don't know how to use that, do y—"

I lifted the weapon and smashed him in the shoulder.
He howled in pain.

Time to end this.

I didn't think. I just tossed the gun aside and tackled my
uncle, landing punch after punch, remembering the dozens

of times I'd felt his fist pound my face, teeth, jaw, and ribs. His drunken rages in the night. His shouting and demeaning and refusal to act like a relative in any way. All the nights I'd gone to bed with a growling stomach and black eye. All those people who'd died in the fire, helpless to escape, terrified as the blaze closed in. And above all . . .

The sound of a blade plunging into my mother's heart.

The headache hit right then, nearly blinding me with its force. Dad hurt Mom, and I killed him for it. Dane *killed* Mom. He deserved a death like none other, and he would receive it at my hand.

Dane lay limp now, half conscious, eyes open but dazed.

I slid my father's knife out of my pocket, nearly dropping it my fingers were so slippery.

Suddenly, Legacy knelt at my side. "Kole," she whispered.

"Hey, give him space," Zenn said, hurrying to pull her away. He looked like he was going to be sick.

She just glowered at him until he backed off. Then she leaned toward me again. "Kole, you already won. We'll make sure he sees justice."

I could feel my heart pounding, rage pumping through my veins along with the blood. It roared in my ears. I felt Zenn's eyes on me, his girlfriend Lorna at his side. Behind him stood an army of Firebrands who watched me with angry frowns. I could barely see them through the haze of anger that gripped me. I stared at Dane's chest, gauging where his heart pumped, grinning at the thought of making it stop.

The headache swelled until I grunted from the pain.

"Stay with me," she said firmly. "You lost your parents to anger. I don't want to lose you too. Please come back."

Dane groaned from the ground. My anger still flowed

like a superpower. I could finish him off right now. I wanted it like I wanted nothing else in this world.

Except Legacy.

The pressure on my head increased until I felt unconsciousness closing in.

"Violence is a poor substitute for justice," she whispered. "Please. Put down the knife."

I stared at the knife, its blade clean and glinting in the too-bright sunlight, my bloody hand gripping the hilt. I noticed my reflection in the metal surface.

How many times had I seen my father hold this very blade in such a way? How many people had met their end just like this, at his hand?

You're just like your dad.

With a massive groan, I threw the knife aside. It bounced and slid to a halt on the grass. Then I fell over next to my uncle, holding my head in my hands to hold off the pain.

Legacy was there in a second, leaning over me. "It's all right," she said, stroking my face. "You did it. They're already taking your uncle away."

I released a low whimper. Second by second, centimeter by centimeter, the pressure began to recede. All I could see was the bright sunlight overhead and Legacy's beautiful face, framed like an angel. My angel.

She cupped my face in her soft hands. "The Firebrands are dragging him away, Kole. They're retreating." She gave me a quick peck on the lips and laughed. "Your uncle will never hurt anyone you love again."

"Mmm," I managed. "That's all well and good, but I'm going to need another one of those. Longer this time."

Her face turned quizzical. "What?"

With great effort, I lifted my hand and pointed to my lips.

She grinned, tucked her hair behind one ear, and covered my lips with hers.

THIRTY-ONE

LEGACY

The press conference began at dusk.

The Block square was filled with smiling people—my supporters from the island, those who had come at Millian's call, Enforcers who had donned their uniforms at the surrender of the Firebrands, and curious onlookers. All signs of battle had been removed hours before, including, thankfully, the macabre evidence of Dane Mason's defeat. It was a moment I didn't want to remember but would never forget.

I smiled at Kole as we sat on the makeshift stand. He'd gained his color back and looked much better, though I detected a deep exhaustion in his eyes. He even wore a new set of clothes some of Dad's assistants brought. Same with Dad. His old clothes made him look more regal despite his still-shaky legs. Alex sat next to him, still wearing his formal clothes and usual frown. I smoothed my own clothing, fully aware that I would be visible behind him. My cheeks ached, but I couldn't stop smiling. This time, I wouldn't have to watch the recording of myself on the IM-NET.

It felt really good.

The only thing that soured this moment was the fact that we'd scoured the city looking for Virgil to no avail. Kole thought he'd be in Malrain by now. I could only hope he was right.

Dad took the stand first. As he did, the audience quieted. No less than fifteen cameras lined the front.

"We all like to think we're making a difference in this world," Dad began. "When you inherit a country by birth, the pressure can be great. I'm sure you can imagine."

The crowd chuckled.

"Before all this began, I thought that what I did made this country better. There's far more to it than people realize, and I got pretty good at juggling it all. The NORA I inherited ran like a dream, thanks to my mother, Her Honorable Treena Hawking." He smiled at the audience. Only then did I realize Gram stood in their midst, covered in a thick coat with the hood pulled up. Nobody seemed to recognize her. Just the way she would want it.

Next to her, Travers hovered like a guard. Our eyes met, his shining with pride and emotion. He thought of his wife, no doubt.

"But then this happened," Dad continued. "I keep thinking that I should have expected this, that I should have done something sooner. Director Virgil's update should never have happened. Neuromen didn't fall under government jurisdiction, but perhaps it should have. Maybe I wouldn't have fallen with many of you and your loved ones had I been more vigilant."

I knew it hurt him to say that. He'd suspected Virgil more than anyone I knew, including me. I'd thought it an obsession back then. He'd been right about everything. Except Virgil's plan turned out to be far worse than anyone expected.

"Then my son took over and received some very bad advice from our enemies," Dad continued, looking at Alex with an apology in his eyes. Next to me, Alex sat staring at the ground. The only indication that he'd heard was the faint pink in his cheeks. "It's amazing how difficult it can be to separate enemies from friends when you're in a position of power. I hope you'll forgive both me and my son." He turned to me. "And then there's my daughter. Legacy could have hidden somewhere and started a new life, but instead, she cared for me while gathering supporters and trying to peacefully win the Block back. Many of you know she barely slept these past weeks. She was too busy trying to negotiate a better future for us, all while fighting against a tide of discouragement. Her decisions weren't perfect either, but as I've watched her fight for you and this nation, I've seen her incredible potential. She inherited the courage of her mother, the stubbornness of her father, and even the confidence of her brother."

With each word, the guilt stabbed deeper. I tried to fake a smile, but even that wouldn't come.

"If I am the last of the tired generation of Hawkings," Dad continued. "Legacy is the beginning of a new. I hereby name her my successor."

Alex gasped.

The crowd leaped to their feet with thunderous applause.

My stomach tumbled to the ground as the words sank in long after they'd registered for everyone else. Dad and Alex had made mistakes, sure, but I'd made the greatest of all— and Dad hadn't even told them.

They would find out eventually. It sent my nerves buzzing.

"I'm pleased with this development," Dad continued,

"enough that I have one more declaration to make. As of today, I'm officially retiring. If Legacy wants me to act as her adviser until she learns her duties, I'll be available between naps." He winked at me, making the crowd laugh. I swallowed the lump in my throat.

Then it hit me. Everyone thought Alex had brought those Malrain soldiers in, and Dad had let them believe it. Eventually, the truth would come out, and I would lose the trust of everyone I cared about.

I couldn't rule if it meant hiding behind a lie.

Dad gestured toward me, encouraging me to take his place behind the mic, but Alex shot to his feet. The audience quieted, looking uncomfortable, as my brother stared at the ground. Then he stalked to the mic and leaned over. Dad took a step to the side. Only the tenseness of his jaw betrayed his worry.

"I have an apology to make," Alex said, his voice echoing across the grounds. He cleared his throat and shifted his feet. "What I did was wrong. I spent years trying to learn what Dad did and watching how people treated him, and, after a while, I wanted them to treat me that way too." He snorted and looked at Dad. "It sounds ridiculous, but I thought taking your position would make me more like you. Instead, it showed the differences between us like a huge stage light. It showed me my family is a greater part of my life than I thought, and I want it to continue that way." He looked at me, his eyes shining with a depth of emotion I hadn't seen in years. "The throne was never meant for me. The events of today make that clearer than ever. I apologize for . . . for bringing the Malrain soldiers here, and I concede to my sister, Legacy Hawking."

I sat frozen in my seat. I couldn't believe it. Alex had taken responsibility for my mistake.

The crowd applauded again, and I could almost feel the entire nation's eyes on me. This all felt too easy. Alex's actions seemed genuine enough, and Dad had dropped everything into my lap whether I wanted it or not. Kole stood at my side and a possible cure for his condition existed somewhere in the world. The Copper Office was mine. So why did I feel an echo of danger deep within my gut?

I looked sideways at the Block we'd reclaimed, trying to make sense of the emotions churning inside me. Was it Kadee's death? The defiling of my father's office? I couldn't quite pinpoint it.

It was then that I saw movement in one of the windows.

I squinted, hoping to see it again. A few seconds later, it reappeared. It was the barrel of a gun—trained not on us or the crowd but on the sky. It jerked and moved as if someone were messing with it.

Or maybe loading it.

"Get everyone to safety," I hissed to Kole. "Shooter in the window." I didn't wait to see his reaction. There wasn't time to send guards in after the shooter, and no stunner would effectively reach that high, even if I had the aim.

But I knew exactly what could.

I leaped from the stage toward the nearest Enforcement vehicle. Behind me, Kole yelled, "Shooter! Everybody hide!"

Screams rose from the crowd as I reached the vehicle. The Enforcers inside blinked. I pounded on the window. "I need your stun cannon!"

They looked at each other in amazement before opening the door and handing it over, the nearest one hefting it in both hands, looking a little dazed. "It's heavy, Your . . . Honor," he finally said.

"Good," I said and stumbled back toward the platform, struggling under the cannon's weight.

Kole had nearly finished scattering the audience, shouting for them to take cover as Enforcers jogged into the building. Now he gestured to Dad and Alex, who seemed to be resisting his warning.

The shooter had his gun loaded now because he began to lower it as I situated the stun cannon against the back of a bench. I shoved the switch on, hearing it whir to life inside. A weird thrill shot through me as it vibrated under my hand. So much power. A tiny screen on the rear read, *Please wait*.

"Come on," I muttered, watching the gun's barrel move as if searching for a target in the dispersing crowd. I couldn't tell who held the weapon in the dimming light, but I had a really good guess.

The cannon vibrated even harder now, still with the same message. I cursed, every second pounding with my racing heart.

Maybe I wouldn't have to use it after all. Maybe those guards would stop him in time.

The shooter's head was visible now, his balding head covered by a combat helmet. But there was no mistaking Virgil's face. Our eyes locked and the man's mouth spread into a victorious grin. The man thought he'd won. But he didn't swing the weapon's barrel around to shoot me as I'd expected.

Instead, he turned back to the stage. The barrel found Dad . . . and stopped.

No, no, no, no, no.

Ready, the screen said.

"You can't have him, *Director*," I breathed, taking aim.

Then I pulled the trigger.

The force of the blast threw me somersaulting backward toward the street. The cannon landed on the ground, narrowly missing crushing my arm.

I lay there, stunned, and stared at the painted sky. A collective groan rose from the remaining crowd. It took all the strength I had to lift my head and find the window. Some of the stone around the window looked cracked, but I saw nothing inside. No weapon, no Virgil.

Seconds later, figures appeared in the window and then disappeared again. Seconds later, someone ran out of the building. "All clear! They caught him."

A collective sigh of relief rose from those still standing nearby. Kole helped me to my feet, glancing at the window every so often to make sure the gun didn't reappear, just in case. Then he helped me walk shakily back to the platform. I brushed my trousers clean, but I refused to sit yet. Kole stood between me and the Block, watching the windows and doors with tense shoulders. An eternity later, several figures emerged from the Block, dragging a still form behind them.

Virgil. Unconscious Virgil. He didn't look nearly as evil with his eyes closed and slumped between four guards. Blood trickled out of each ear, and he wore what promised to be an incredible bruise on his face.

I cringed and stepped down from the platform to talk to the guards. "Is he alive?"

"Yes, Your Honor," one of the guards said, grunting under the weight. "Probably burst his eardrums, though, and he may have a concussion. Where would you like him?"

"A prison cell. We'll send a physician to check on him." I didn't trust Virgil to be contained by hospital security for a second. "And send another team to clear the building. We don't need any more scares like that."

The guards nodded and dragged Virgil away.

"Goodbye, Director Virgil," I muttered. If I had any say, he'd be seeing the inside of that prison cell for a really, *really* long time.

Dad jogged up, looking pale and shaky, and wrapped his arms around me. "That was far too close. I keep learning not to underestimate that man."

"But why shoot you and not me?" I asked into his shoulder.

"Because he knows I would have hunted him down. I would never let Virgil wander the planet while my daughter ruled. He's tried to destroy my family too many times, and that is unforgivable." The steel in Dad's voice softened into a chuckle. "After a shot like that, though, you'd better believe he'll wish he'd targeted a different Hawking."

As I pulled away from Dad, grinning, Kole joined me. "Well, if you meant to impress everyone even more, you just did. I think you can go claim the Copper Office now."

Alex reached us, his frown slightly less deep than usual. He gave Kole a glare before nudging my shoulder with his own. "Go get it, sis."

"I intend to," I said, "but first I have a speech to make."

Dad looked at me quizzically. "Now? Are you sure?"

"Yes." A new flutter of anxiety welled up inside me. Why was it easier to shoot the stun cannon at a murderer than give a speech? Especially the one I knew I had to make. "But first, I need you to answer one question. Are you sure about this?"

"I am." He looked deep into my eyes as if seeing my doubts and insecurities and everything else I kept hidden inside. "No matter what you do next, I support you. I'm sure Mom would too."

I looked at Alex. He gave a tiny nod.

"Family before country," Dad said, correcting his creed. He gave my shoulder a squeeze and took his seat again. I stood where he'd left me, still feeling where he'd gripped my shoulder, and felt warm inside like I hadn't in a very long time.

The audience quieted as I gripped the sides of the podium to steady myself. Two roads lay before me now, and one felt brighter and lighter than the other. But it would take more courage than I had now to say what I needed to say.

I searched the audience and found Millian in the crowd. She clasped her hands near her face in utter joy. Her happiness was for me, her friend. Would she still speak to me after this speech? There was only one way to find out.

"I met a little boy recently," I began. "He taught me a few things. I'd like to share them with you now."

The silence felt like a weight of its own, filling the empty air around us. I had everyone's attention.

"When I was born, I had two different mothers. One gave me birth but could give me nothing else. The other offered a life withheld from most children in the world— wealth, luxury. My own room. Elaborate dinners, closets full of designer clothes, an education, a future. She gave me her heart, her family. Herself." My voice was strangled. This was no way to begin. I took a second to clear my throat before continuing, noting a couple of members of the audience dabbing at their eyes. "There's only one thing she couldn't offer me, and I'm realizing now that it's something the Hawking family has forever promised but never quite delivered. Freedom.

"The Rating system was designed to keep citizens from inequality. There would be no more unfair poverty or wealth, they said. If a person was either one, it would be because they chose it. Gram—er, my grandmother discovered otherwise. It seems conspiracies, like weeds in a rich flowerbed, can never quite be abolished. There will always be someone grabbing for power. And most of the time, that power comes at a cost. Usually, the cost is freedom. Even my own family has paid a heavy price for it. Today, we've all shared that price."

I caught Gram's eyes in the crowd. Her eyes glistened with unshed tears.

I lifted my chin, more sure of my path now. "I come before you as the only person in this land with true freedom, and I offer it to you now. Take it. Be smarter with it than we were. In swinging away from the Rating system, we created a system nearly as problematic. The truth remains somewhere in the middle. So I declare that there will no longer be a bloodline ruler in NORA. From this moment on, your leaders will be elected by popular vote—and every single graduate will have a vote. Never allow anyone to take it from you again."

Behind me, Alex sounded as if he was choking. I didn't dare turn around. Instead, I smiled at the cameras, watching them swim in my blurry vision.

"The Hawking family will forever be in your debt. We thank you for allowing us to serve you. It has been the greatest honor of my life, and I'm sure my family can say the same."

All eyes turned to Dad. I turned as slowly as possible, sure I would see the same horror in him that I'd seen at my Declaration a few months back. I'd just taken his job and everything else away from him. I'd ended the bloodline ruling system and, with it, removed every ounce of his power.

But the father I saw before me now was far from the

same man. He trembled as he straightened his shoulders, looking lighter than he had in years, and nodded. He returned to my side. "I, too, thank you for the trust you've placed in us. I will support my daughter's edict."

My edict. It sounded so official when he said it that way. I threw my arms around him, partly holding him up at this point. "Thank you."

"No," he said softly. "Thank *you*."

THIRTY-TWO

KOLE

I SAT in a too-soft chair under heavy lights that made every pore in my body sweat. I shifted my weight to find a comfortable position. The interview set had a distinct feminine flair—a sofa with floral pillows, some kind of metal climby thing with plants growing all over it, a stack of fake books on the coffee table. Across the room, in the darker section, Legacy chatted excitedly with Millian. Foster, Legacy's former assistant, had planted himself right next to Millian, their fingers intertwined. Millian gave him a shy smile, and he grinned back.

I chuckled. They hadn't been exactly shy when we'd caught them making out in the transport a few minutes before. It reminded me of the first kiss Legacy and I shared —hot and fast and life-changing. Even now, months later, that same heat rushed through me, and I longed for this to be over so we could be alone together again.

"Two minutes," the reporter said, sitting down in her chair. I'd never seen this one before. A new hire, then. Something that would have been impossible under Malachi's or Alex Hawking's reign just one month earlier.

Legacy hurried across the room to join us. I immediately pulled her close and leaned down to whisper in her ear. "Should we open this interview by showing Millian and Foster how kissing is done?"

"That would certainly improve the ratings," she teased, but the tiniest blush appeared in her cheeks.

"Later, then."

She grinned. "That's a given."

Legacy wore a stylish pair of trousers and a dark-red blouse I was sure had been her mother's. It brought out the warmth in her brown hair and the brightness in her brown eyes, and I couldn't tear my eyes from her. Neither would the rest of the country, I knew, once this interview began.

She leaned over to whisper again. "I still don't understand why Millian isn't going first. Nobody wants to hear from me."

"You're the opening act, and I'm your sidekick. No pressure or anything."

"Have I ever told you how much I hate cameras?" she moaned, nodding as the reporter held up her forefinger. One minute.

"Better get used to this. I hear the second-in-command gives a lot of speeches. I also hear the second-in-command's consort gives hardly any, which suits me just fine."

"There's never been a second-in-command before."

"Exactly."

She elbowed me in the side, making me grunt.

The reporter's eyebrows lifted, making her entire face light up, as someone counted down across the room. Then it was time.

All business now, the reporter smiled at the camera. "We're here with our nation's favorite couple, Legacy Hawking and Kole Mason—former heiress and former scientist from the Shadows. It's a modern version of the Cinderella story, wouldn't you say?"

"If you reverse it, maybe," Legacy said, looking at me sideways. "Although I don't think Kole would look very good in a dress."

I snorted.

"You two are positively delightful," the reporter said. "It's a pleasure to be here with you both. It's been one month to the day since your announcement, Legacy. We all know what's happened since then. Were you surprised when your best friend was elected to take your place?"

"Not in the least," she said easily. "In fact, I think everyone got that exactly right. I can't think of anyone more suited to lead a country."

"Did you expect to come in second?"

"I didn't expect to come in anything. I figured the country was tired of Hawkings leading them, and I was fine with stepping down. But I'm honored to be entrusted with such an important role."

"Even though you originally shunned it?" the reporter prompted.

"Yes. And when it's time for me to be replaced, I hope I'll be able to say I did my best and the country is better for my service."

"I'm sure I speak for everyone when I say we're truly grateful to you, Miss Hawking. Now, you had a single request for your successor, and we've already seen it fulfilled. Why did you feel so strongly about restoring the border cities to Malrain?"

Legacy spoke easily, confidently. "Because they were never ours in the first place. Malrain killed a lot of innocent people at the Block, but we've taken just as many of their lives in the past. And yes, they tried to take our country, but we took part of theirs first. We've spent the past decades condemning them for what we ourselves have done, and it isn't fair. It's time to end the fighting and restore peace as we should have all along."

"Some are critical of the new border," the reporter said, pasting on a serious expression. "They feel like they've had their homes stolen from them."

Legacy didn't miss a beat. "Just as the Malrain settlers felt in the beginning. But Her Honorable Millian Comondor has been generous enough to provide new homes for them within the border. I think their quality of life will be much better now that the fighting is over."

"Is that the reason for the new trade agreements as well?"

"You'll have to ask Millian about that, but I agree with her decision 100 percent. Malrain are no longer our enemies. They're our neighbors. They have resources and knowledge to share with us and vice versa. We can learn from one another."

"You clearly have a deep sense of right and wrong. Is that the reason you had a hospital worker arrested recently? Did he have something to do with the attempted takeover at the Block?"

"In a way," she said. "I owed it to someone, and now everything is as it should be."

The reporter looked disappointed at the vague answer but quickly hid it. She turned to me. "Kole, you once Declared for Neuromen, but it was recently announced that the lab will not be rebuilt. What are your plans now?"

"I've always had an interest in tech engineering," I said. "I'm hoping to intern at a company across town. They originally offered me a position there, and I'm glad they still believe I'm capable of fulfilling their needs." I still felt a little dumbstruck about it, to be honest. The position offered a decent living, but even more, recent changes made it so I could climb quickly in the company. No tattoos, oaths, or fistfights necessary. Just hard work and skill.

Mom would have been proud.

"That's secondary to my real job, though," I continued, squeezing Legacy's hand. "I plan to be here for Legacy however and whenever she needs me. And she will. Don't let her fool you." I winked at the cameras.

The reporter turned back to Legacy. "He seems like a good one."

Legacy laughed. "The best."

"Your family home, though," the reporter continued, growing serious again as she addressed Legacy. "There have been rumors that your family has moved out and construction vehicles have been spotted out front."

"True and true. It's being renovated." She looked at me, and I watched her, nodding my encouragement. She took a deep breath. "I guess now is as good a time to announce it as any. My family won't be living there again. With only three of us and two fully grown, it's time to move on."

When Legacy didn't continue, the reporter leaned forward eagerly. "What will it be, then, a museum? Surely your family has a fascinating political history full of artifacts of interest to future generations."

"We thought about that," Legacy admitted, her blush apparent. "But there's something we need even more than that. We're turning it into a refuge for the poor. They'll have a warm place to sleep, food to eat, and support to learn the skills they need for a good job. But that isn't all." She paused. "We have three more planned in cities across the country."

The reporter actually gasped. "That's remarkable. What a benevolent gift."

"Thanks, but it shouldn't be considered a gift. The citizens of NORA paid for our home, and I can't think of a better use for it. I just wish we could renovate these buildings faster and get children off the streets."

"You and Her Honorable Millian Comondor have done a good job of finding temporary housing for the homeless during the past weeks," the reporter said. "You haven't announced it, but we've been watching. Thank you for your humble service."

"It's my pleasure, truly."

"Once you and Her Honor discovered how to permanently disable Virgil's brain implants, recovery rates shot upward. Only a small percentage of our original comatose patients remain hospitalized. I'm sure you're glad to see that as well."

"That was all Millian. I'm devastated for those we lost but very grateful for the ones we were able to save. We have a long road of recovery ahead, though—physically and otherwise."

"Agreed. Thanks to you, we'll do it together." The reporter turned back to me, her eyebrows lifted in mock innocence. "Rumors say that you once supported the Rating system, Kole Mason. What is your feeling on that now?"

I barked a laugh. This particular question had to be Gram's doing. The woman would be watching on the handheld device I'd made for her, blankets piled high in her lap. "It's no secret that I was a Firebrand once. Like the others, and like many of you, I wanted a better life. I thought the Rating system could bring us that. But I was wrong, because the Rating system would have cost us just as many lives as it did the first time. Legacy saw that. She knew what changes *really* needed to be made and she made them, not caring what she would lose as a result. I suspect that's why you voted her onto the cabinet. You see what I see in her—a good heart."

"Speaking of which," the reporter said with a sly look, "What are your intentions with our second-in-command?"

I looked down on Legacy, who tensed. "Are you kidding? I'm definitely marrying her."

Now, it was Legacy who gasped. Across the room, Millian giggled.

The reporter clapped her hands before gathering her composure once more. "You're sure she'll say yes?"

"I'm no dummy. I'll work on her till she does." And thanks to the medicine Malrain gave her as a thank-you gift, I would be around for as long as it took to convince her. I even had our place picked out on the island, an abandoned home in near-perfect condition near a grassy field along the empty coastline.

A slow grin spread across Legacy's face. "That may not be as much work as you think."

Desire shot through my veins like a live electrical wire, but I only planted a chaste kiss on her hair. We were on national news, after all. Despite my earlier joking, I wasn't about to embarrass her the way her ex-boyfriend had. She'd had quite enough of that in her lifetime.

Legacy rolled her eyes, placed a hand behind my head, and pulled my face to hers for a kiss that left no question where she stood.

The entire room erupted in whooping and delightful laughter. The reporter clapped her hands to her thighs as we finished and looked back at the camera, Legacy sitting with her hands folded sweetly in her lap, and me . . . Well, I wouldn't be okay for a while. My hair was messed up now, for one thing, and I was almost positive my face matched Legacy's blouse.

"A Cinderella story if I've ever seen one," the reporter repeated, her voice still bouncing with laughter. She turned back to the cameras. "The nation's Second Couple, ladies and gentlemen. May it be a true beginning and a happy ending all at once."

Legacy smiled at me, her eyes sharp and happy and full of promise. She took my hand in hers. "I'm pretty sure it already is."

If you loved the Numbers Game Saga, other readers want to know about it. Please consider leaving a quick review. Thank you!

LIKE FANTASY AND PIRATES?

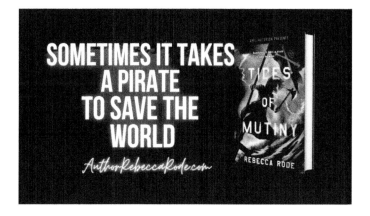

Decades ago, a band of female pirates nearly conquered the world. Now the king executes female sailors—which complicates Laney's dream of becoming captain. She must disguise herself as a boy in order to survive.

But when the king's son asks Laney to help him save his father's kingdom, Laney must embrace the danger of discovery for the possibility for the life she's always wanted.

It's time to pull off a mutiny of her own.

WHAT TO READ NEXT: FLICKER

Ember knows three things for certain.

- She sees the future.
- They want to turn her into the galaxy's deadliest weapon.
- Even the strongest weapons can backfire.

If you love epic space sagas, experience Flicker now!

ABOUT THE AUTHOR

REBECCA RODE is a *USA Today* and *Wall Street Journal* bestselling author. Her published fiction includes the Numbers Game Saga, the Ember in Space trilogy, and TIDES OF MUTINY (Little, Brown Young Readers). She has also published nonfiction and online news articles for several publications, but she prefers writing for teens and the young at heart. She is represented by Kelly Peterson at Rees Literary. Visit Rebecca at AuthorRebeccaRode.com.

Printed in Great Britain
by Amazon